Impetuous R.,
Secret Agent

By Jane Leslie Conly

Illustrated by Bonnie Leick

HYPERION BOOKS FOR CHILDREN · NEW YORK

AN IMPRINT OF DISNEY BOOK GROUP

First Edition

10 9 8 7 6 5 4 3 2 1

Designed by Eileen Gilshian

Printed in the United States of America

This book is set in 12-point Mrs. Eaves.

Library of Congress Cataloging-in-Publication Data on file.

ISBN 978-1-4231-0418-6

Reinforced binding

Visit www.hyperionbooksforchildren.com

To Eliza, my inspiration

Impetuous R.,
Secret Agent

❧

CHAPTER ONE

Urgent Meeting

SHINY, IMPY, AND DEMOSTHENES ROACH were
out of roach school for the summer, and they were celebrating. They were an odd trio: Demosthenes, or Demo,
was tall and shy; Impy was short and talkative; and Shiny
was almost always dancing. Now they were on their way to
a game of kick-the-crumb, to be held, Impy explained,
"under the southeast side of the loose molding in the
storeroom of Pop's Corner, a jazz club on Washington
Avenue in the neighborhood of Melbourn in the city of
Baltimore, Maryland, USA, Planet Earth." Impy, short
for Impetuous, almost never thought about what he

was going to say or do ahead of time, which occasionally led to trouble. But Shiny thought he was funny.

"Shut up, Imp," she said, laughing. Demo just stood there. Then Shiny noticed a sign posted behind the refrigerator, right above the hole that the roaches passed through on their way to the basement. "'Urgent Meeting,'" she read out loud. The words were printed not in English but in Roach script, a form of writing created back in the ancient times by the insect group Blattodea, which has survived for more than three hundred million years and has species on every continent except Antarctica. So taught Socra-Roach, the elder, who lectured on roach history every Monday morning during the school year. Thank goodness *that* was over, Shiny thought.

"What kind of meeting?" Impy asked. "Where is it? And why's it so important?"

"Behind this refrigerator at two o'clock," a sultry voice answered. "But you won't be there."

"Carlita!" cried Shiny.

Carlita had caught them by surprise. She was a petite roach with a bright green shell. As usual, her two hind legs were moving to some unheard beat.

"Why not?" Impy asked, because Shiny was agog and couldn't speak. Carlita was so beautiful! Shiny was part of the same species, the Green Banan, but because she was young, her shell was still a dusty brown.

"The meeting's about a grown-up problem. We don't want you nymphs getting upset." Carlita hurried on, intent on some errand. But her answer was all the three young roaches needed to hear.

"We'll be there," Impy said. "Only, they won't see us, because we'll be absolutely, positively certain that we are—"

"Hidden." Shiny nodded.

Demo just stood there.

"Excitement!" Impy jumped up and down. "Action! Cameras!"

"We don't have cameras," Shiny said.

"We can build one! And then—"

"Late." Demo tucked the crumb ball into the other side of his cheek and led the others down the wallpaper and around the corner, where their teammates were waiting.

There were more than five hundred young roaches living at Pop's Corner, at last count. They came from four families: the family of Socra-Roach, which counted its heritage from the days of the ancient Greeks; the Green Banans, who had traveled to Baltimore in the guitar case of a young musician; the family of Madagascar hissing cockroaches, called Maddies, famous for their massive size; and last but not least, the Harlequin family, who had beautiful striped shells and tended toward patience and tranquillity. There was mixing between families, so that a nymph like Demo might have a father descended from Socra-Roaches and a mother from the island of Madagascar. Shiny's heritage was mostly Green Banan. Impy was a mix of Harlequin and someone from the garbage cans in the alley, so that now and then the other youngsters broke the rules and called him Mutt. To add insult to injury, he was the runt of his litter and had remained unusually small. So he spent a lot of time trying to prove just how important he really was.

CHAPTER TWO

Trouble at Pop's

SOCRA-ROACH STOOD at the podium, a tiny slab of
wood on the wall behind the refrigerator. His audience lay
in layers on the back coils of the refrigerator. They formed
an undulating mass of heads and legs, shells and antennae.

"What is coming?" the old roach asked.

"A party?"

He shook his head.

"A visitor?"

"No."

"Trouble—" somebody guessed.

Socra-Roach waggled his walking stick to show that

that was correct. He addressed the crowd:

"Today we face the biggest crisis in our history at Pop's Corner."

"What could it possibly be?" Impy whispered. He, Shiny, and Demo had scrunched into a sliver of space under the peeling linoleum floor. They could hear everything, but had to take turns sticking their heads out and reporting on what they saw.

Socra-Roach was known for taking his time before he arrived at the crux of a situation. "We all have our own reasons for living here," he went on. "But I think we mostly agree that Pop's Corner is a splendid home for roaches: dark, with many crumbs, and—because it is a bar instead of a restaurant—no health inspection."

The words *health inspection* sent a shudder through the crowd. Socra-Roach continued: "We know also that Pops has always cared more about music than cleanliness or money. For years, his wife, Earlene, paid the club's bills. When she grew ill this spring, many of us hoped their son, Charlie, would step into the breach. But since he opened his law office in March, he's been so busy that he hasn't paid attention to what's going on. Instead he deposits the *grandkids* here as often as he can, with the excuse of cheering Pops and Mama up."

"Uhhhhgg . . . the grandkids." Most of the crowd was dismissive, but Impy and Shiny poked each other, because they found the human children fascinating.

"Predictably, the bills have not been paid. This morning, Pops had a meeting with an officer from the bank. It was downtown, but I took the liberty of sneaking

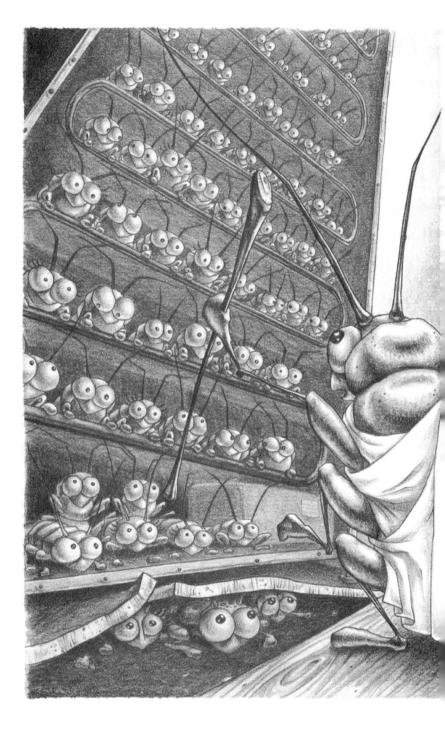

into Pops's jacket lining so I could attend."

The roaches strained forward, eager to know what had happened. When it was Impy's turn to look, he got so excited that instead of peeking, he jumped completely out of the hole. He was spotted immediately. A guardian signaled for Socra-Roach to wait. She was a Maddie, and she tossed Impy lightly over her huge chestnut-colored back and headed toward the nursery.

"I want to know the problem!" Impy shouted. "I have to know! I want to help!"

"Patience, patience," murmured the Harlequins.

Shiny and Demo tunneled farther under the linoleum.

Socra-Roach waited until the disturbance was over. Then he continued: "The bank officer told Pops that he owes seven thousand dollars on unpaid loans. There's also a four-thousand-dollar tax bill from the IRS. If Pops doesn't repay these debts within forty-five days, the club will be auctioned off to someone else."

"*Someone else!*" The Maddies began to hiss. Their great bodies swayed back and forth, almost knocking the smaller roaches through the refrigerator coils.

Socra-Roach raised his walking stick. "Be reasonable!" he pleaded. "Control yourselves."

"We'll be doomed! Dead! Destroyed!"

But, after a moment, the Maddie roaches started to calm down. Slowly their hisses faded.

When it was quiet, the elder continued: "Our fates are in our own feet, and so, if I may remind you, are the fates of Pops and Earlene Wiggins, who have so kindly sheltered us for all these years."

There was silence while the audience remembered the loving times provided by the old man. His wife was nice too, except that she didn't like roaches coming into her and Pops's upstairs apartment, and she called modern jazz "that noise."

Carlita loved music, especially jazz. Now she made up a song:

> *"If we die,*
> *We'll zombies be,*
> *Dancing in the jazz clubs*
> *of history. . . ."*

"*Deeeaaaaad . . .*" the Maddie roaches hissed.

"Patience," the Harlequins answered. "Life will unfold just as it should."

CHAPTER THREE

The Outside World

"SO EMBARRASSING! Absolutely, positively, the most embarrassing incident of my entire life!" Impy moaned. "To be carried out like a nymph not yet hatched from its mother's egg sack."

"Shut up, Imp," Shiny said, twirling the bit of silver ribbon tied to her antennae. "We want to tell you what happened."

Demo just stood there.

"All right!" Impy said. "Tell!"

Shiny did, adding at the very end, "If someone doesn't come up with the money, all of us will have to move!"

"*Move*? But the awful stories . . ."

Shiny nodded. "I know."

"Like how my cousin's family almost got killed by poison spray at the convention center, and then a cat ate some of us alive in Fells Point, and afterward the people in the suburbs were so mean and selfish that they threw their crumbs down that horrible thing called a garbage disposal. . . .

"And how the tour ship began to sink in the Atlantic, and they put the humans onto rafts, but let the roaches drown. . . .

"And how they put those pretty crystals on the floor for us to taste, but then it turned out they were—"

"Shut up, Imp!" Shiny pointed. While they were talking, Demo had panicked. He swayed back and forth, then collapsed in a dead faint.

They sprinkled water on his face. He came to, gasping and shaking his head wildly.

"It's okay, Demo. We're going to figure out a plan so we can stay at Pops's."

Demo was still upset.

Shiny sang a lyric from a rock-and-roll song she'd heard once on the radio: *"It's all all right! It's all all right!"*

"Maybe or maybe not," Impy muttered under his breath. But luckily, the others didn't hear.

CHAPTER FOUR

Scoping the Joint

THEY HAD THEIR OWN MEETING inside the loose pipe fitting under the kitchen sink.

"The question is, where can we get money? And not just a little money—thousands and thousands of dollars."

"Or help Pops get it," Shiny said.

Demo just stood there.

"First we should think of the places money is kept," Impy said. He counted them off on his legs: "Banks, and cash registers, and armored cars, and wallets, and—"

"Checkbooks," Shiny said. "And ATM cards. Then there's traveler's checks—you know what the ads say: 'As good as cash.'" Shiny sometimes hid under the reclining chair in Pops's apartment to watch TV. There was a television in the bar too, but the music made it hard to hear.

"Those are good." Impy was writing them down. "Anything else?"

"Diamonds are worth money. So are gold and art and antiques—"

"Whoa," Impy said. "Pops is old. Do you think he has antiques?"

"Those velvet paintings of the golden age of jazz are nice, but I don't know how valuable they are."

"So we ought to go upstairs and look around." Impy sighed. "The problem is that we'll be breaking rule number six: no nymphs allowed in Pops and Earlene's apartment."

Shiny started rapping:

> *"Rules, rules, rules . . .*
> *rules are for fools,*
> *but we're no fools,*
> *we're outta school,*
> *we're cool, so cool,*
> *we rule. . . ."*

She finished with a twirl and a bow.

"I think this is a bad idea, Shiny."

But Impy followed her up the kitchen wall, and Demo followed after.

The apartment was off-limits to all but the oldest and most careful roaches, because Earlene didn't want any bugs there, and when she saw one, she got upset. Sometimes she threatened to put down poison, and she always fussed at Pops: "You spend all your time downstairs listening to noise, while this place is crawling with roaches!"

"Sorry, dear," Pops would mumble. Sometimes he'd hug Earlene or pat her hand. Then she'd forgive him. But whether she forgave Pops or not, the roaches had to be extremely careful.

Nevertheless, some of the youngsters had visited the apartment secretly, to see what it was like. Earlene was a tidy housekeeper, so there were never any crumbs on the floor or counters, but if you could make it into her garbage can, the leftovers were wonderful: pieces of biscuit and cake and salad and bacon and cornbread and deviled eggs. But they were dangerous to get to, because if Earlene happened to see you crossing the kitchen floor, she would try her best to step on you! In this way more than one tragedy had befallen the colony. Each incident was followed by grieving, after which there were the same warnings: "Keep away from the apartment! It is Pops's private domain. He doesn't invade our homes, and it is only fair and just that we not invade his."

The three friends scuttled up the wallpaper pattern. Shiny knew just where she was going. She stopped the other two in the dark angle where two walls came together and whispered, "This is what they call the living room."

"Ooohhh . . ." Impy liked the look of the big comfortable chairs, with soft lighting from above. The lounge downstairs was nearly always dim, and the seats were made of wood.

"Come on, I'll take you to the bedroom. That's where Earlene stays since she got sick. I'll bet Pops is in there too."

The trip to the bedroom took time. The shortest route was right across the ceiling, but Shiny said they didn't dare. So they scurried one by one along the molding, staying behind hutches and cupboards whenever they could. Eventually they reached an open door.

"Careful." Shiny led the other two around the corner, then scuttled under the bottom edge of a large bookcase. Her friends followed on foot.

Impy gagged: "The dust—"

"Shhhh . . . she's been too sick to clean."

They climbed the wall behind the bureau until they reached the top. "Don't say a word," Shiny whispered. Then all three poked their heads, antennae first, over the back edge of the dresser.

This is what they saw: a soft, pretty, white-haired lady in a pink bathrobe. She was sitting up in bed, with a tray across her lap. On it were a plate, a cup, a pair of glasses, a book, and a remote control. In a chair beside the bed sat Pops himself. Today he was wearing old pants with baggy knees, a striped sweater, and as usual, a battered brown fedora hat.

"So I'll get your medicine, and pick up the groceries, and come back and put them away. Then Zeena's coming over with Troy and Bitty. . . ."

"My grandbabies." Earlene beamed.

"I'll have to get the show ready—the band is coming in at eight."

"Don't forget the bills. You've been telling me for days that you were going to pay them."

"Let me worry about money. You're supposed to be thinking about getting well."

"I am a *little* better, don't you think, Herbert?"

"Sure you are . . ." Pops leaned over and kissed his wife on the cheek. But when he turned away, the three roaches could see that his eyes looked terribly sad.

CHAPTER FIVE

The Grandkids

CHESTER, TROY, AND NICOLE—usually called Bitty—
were feared by the adult roaches because each of them had
passed through a phase when they loved to hear the crunch
and snap of roach shells underfoot. But Chester was now a
freshman at Princeton, far too dignified to chase or trample
roaches; and Troy, eleven, had turned into a quiet, sensitive
boy who wouldn't hurt a flea. Bitty was a different matter.

Bitty had been exceptional since the day she was born.
She had weighed only four pounds when the nurse first set
her, howling and wiggling, on the infant scale; and now,
approaching her fifth birthday, she was tiny compared to

other kids her age. Her features were delicate, and with her halo of dark hair, some people said she looked like an angel. Others mistook her for a toddler, and because of this—or maybe just because she liked to—she often behaved like one. Pops and Earlene adored Bitty, but they both realized that she needed limits.

It made sense for the roaches to be afraid of Bitty. Not only was she dangerous—her shoes were leather with hard soles—she was also unpredictable. One minute she could be sitting on the floor playing peacefully with her baby doll, and the next she might jump up and down and shriek: "Grandpa! Grandmama! Come right now!!" If her grandparents didn't obey her commands, she would scream louder, until the air shook with the power of her voice. If Pops and Earlene *still* didn't come, Bitty would lie down on her back and cry delicate little tears, which formed roach lakes on the tavern floor. There was only one way to change her mood: turn on the music. Then Bitty would leap up and start to dance.

Today's visit was typical. Troy and Bitty were dropped off around noon, while the trio of young roaches was still hiding behind Earlene's bureau. The kids' mom, Zeena, had her briefcase in her hand. She gave both in-laws and children a kiss and hurried off to a meeting. Troy and Bitty ate doughnuts and drank milk with their grandmother and watched cartoons. Then they asked if they could go down to the lounge to visit Grandpa.

Shiny spun around and headed downstairs. She didn't want to miss a minute of spying on Bitty, whom she found fascinating. Impy and Demo were more interested in Troy, whose

gentle ways were less alarming. The roaches arrived on the ceiling of the club just as the kids found Pops starting to work on the sound system.

"Grandpa, want me to plug this in?" Troy was eager to please.

"No, me!"

"Bitty, I asked first."

"No, me!"

"Bitty, let Troy do it. You're too little."

Bitty hated the fact that she was smaller than other kids, and each time it was brought up she had a tantrum. Now she flung herself onto the floor and punched the air with her thin, delicate legs. Carefully, Troy stepped around her and plugged in the speaker wires. At first Pops pretended she wasn't there.

"No fair! No fair! It's my turn!!"

"What I meant was, you're too *young* to handle electricity,"

Pops said. "Now, get up off the floor, Bitty. We have wires to lay."

"Can I help?"

"Yes, you can dust the speakers." Pops winked at Troy and handed Bitty his handkerchief. She worked with great enthusiasm. Dust clouds flew so high that up on the ceiling they tickled Impy's nose and made him want to sneeze.

"Shhhh . . ." Shiny warned.

Demo just stood there.

"I'm done."

"How about dusting the bar?"

She ran to do it.

"Got to keep her busy," Pops whispered. He beamed at his favorite grandson. Troy giggled.

The two worked companionably. Pops would sing a tune and Troy filled in the harmony.

"Did you ask your dad about those music lessons?" Pops asked, after a while.

"He said soon. Wants me to be old enough to know I'll practice, because he didn't, and the lesson money was wasted."

"That's for sure. But that may have been all right, 'cause they say talent always skips a generation."

"What did you play, Grandpa?"

"Trumpet. And I learned it from the greatest."

Troy had heard this story many times, but he egged Pops on anyway. "Who was that?"

"The master—Louis Armstrong." Pops paused. "Way back in the nineteen thirties and forties this part of Baltimore was famous for jazz. There were clubs all up and down Wabash Avenue. Even though this place was off the main route, the owner was a famous drummer, Maxy Bishop. Before he retired and bought the club, Maxy had played with all the greats. So when they went on tour, this was a regular stop. All the big names played here. Artie Shaw brought Billie Holiday, not when she was starting out, but after people were lining up for blocks to hear her sing. Louis Armstrong knew Maxy, too. He'd come play every year, and when he did, people from all over the city would pile into this place until there wasn't an inch left to stand in. The ladies would wear furs and diamonds and heels as high as stilts. The men would smoke cigars. Nowadays people don't like that, but back then it was the mark of a gentleman to smoke a good cigar."

"But how did you *meet* Louis Armstrong, Grandpa?"

"I was doing setup for Maxy, just like we're doing now, and Louis Armstrong came in early—wanted to have a drink with his old friend before the show began. Maxy had a flat tire on his way to the club, so I sat Mr. Armstrong down and fetched him a cold beer. He asked me why I was working at the club, and I told him I loved jazz—especially the trumpet. He took his own instrument out of the case and asked to hear me play. Standing there in front of him, I was so nervous I could hardly make a sound.

"He didn't embarrass me, though. He just took the trumpet back and showed me a couple of tricks."

"How old were you?"

"Just a few years older than you. Of course my folks didn't have the money for college, so I—"

"ALL DONE!" Bitty appeared from nowhere.

Pops sighed. It seemed like he never got through a story with his granddaughter around. But Troy smiled at his little sister. "How about scrubbing out the bar sink and wiping the counter down? Then Grandpa won't have to do it tonight."

"I already do'd it!" The handkerchief was filthy, but Bitty didn't care.

"I *did* it," Troy corrected gently.

But by then she was gone.

CHAPTER SIX

Ideas

"HUNGRY," DEMO SAID. He was a roach of few words. Impy and Shiny accepted that, for Maddie nymphs were often late bloomers. Now Demo followed Shiny and Impy down from the ceiling in search of food. They found a sizable crumb on the floor behind the radiator and broke it into three portions. "Potato chip!" That was one of Demo's favorites. Shiny preferred popcorn, but she chowed down happily, content from her observations of Troy and Bitty. Impy watched in disgust.

"Eat, eat, eat! That's all you two think about."

"Shut up," Shiny said, but her mouth was full of food.

Demo just stood there.

"I won't shut up! We have a problem to solve—a huge problem. We can't let ourselves be distracted by material needs like food." Impy could hardly wait till Shiny swallowed her last bite.

"What did you think of Pops's furniture?"

"Not like anything on *Antiques Roadshow*."

"How about the necklace on the bureau?"

"I checked—it's plastic."

"There can't be extra cash. If there were, Pops would have used it to pay the bills."

Shiny nodded. "*And* we know Earlene has no idea the club is broke."

"I bet Pops kept it a secret so she wouldn't get upset."

"Has he told Charlie? He might have savings. . . ."

"I don't think so. Opening that law office cost more than they expected. And last year, when Chester got into Princeton, Charlie said the tuition would empty out their savings account." Secretly Impy'd wished that he could go to Princeton too, in Chester's backpack. But when he'd asked his mother, she'd said no.

Shiny was dancing the polka and twirling the gold ribbons on her antennae to the beat. "We could try the lottery." She spun around in circles. "The TV says that if you play, you win."

Impy shook his head. He'd been at Socra-Roach's lesson on gambling. The class had figured out the odds and concluded that the chances of winning the lottery were very, very small.

"Then how about robbing a bank?" Shiny's moral

leanings were, at times, relative to the situation. "We could steal cash or traveler's checks! It will only take—"

"We could *borrow* the money from the bank," Impy thought out loud.

"Who would lend money to roaches?"

"Or else," Impy said, catching Shiny's drift, "we could make a human borrow it for us."

"How could we *make* it? They're bigger and stronger than we are. And once it had the money, it might step on us."

"No." Impy shook his head. "Because we'd be holding something valuable—something it wanted back."

"Shut up, Imp."

"Nope," Demo said.

There was silence—perhaps even discouragement. Impy began to wonder what his mother was making for supper. Demo stared at his antennae as if they'd suddenly become extremely interesting. Shiny twitched her ribbons to the right, then left, in a silent dance. Suddenly she stopped, rolled backward, flipped over, and jumped onto her hind feet. She stuck her other four legs into the air and waved them all at once.

"You know how they have parties—benefits—to raise money? And rock stars sing and play music? Couldn't we do that for Pops?"

Impy was dubious. "People wouldn't pay to see *us* perform. Remember, to them we're pests. They have no idea—"

"I wasn't suggesting that *we* perform. I meant we could invite human celebrities. Who's the one Pops is always talking about? Louis Armstrong?"

Impy nodded slowly. Maybe Shiny had a good idea after all. "It does sound like they're old friends. If Louis knew that Pops was in trouble, he'd probably come running as fast as he could!"

"How can we let him know?" Shiny asked.

"We'll write him a letter."

"That's a wonderful idea! Shall we vote on it?"

Impy followed the procedure in Roaches' Rules of Order: "State the proposal, please."

"That we write a letter to Louis Armstrong asking him to play a benefit concert at the club."

"All in favor?"

"Aye." Shiny nodded.

"Aye." Demo nodded.

"Aye." Impy nodded.

"So it's unanimous. When shall we begin?"

"Tonight!"

The nymphs agreed to meet in Pops's office after he'd gone upstairs to bed.

CHAPTER SEVEN

၆‌ၡၟ

Forty-four Days Left, and Counting . . .

WRITING THE LETTER turned out to be harder than the
nymphs had imagined. Writing materials were kept in Pops's
desk, top left drawer, which was closed. That meant Shiny,
Impy, and Demo had to construct an upside-down lever to
open it. They slid a Popsicle stick into the drawer handle,
stood on the edge of the desk with Demo in front and the
others holding on behind, and pulled back with all their
might. Luckily the drawer didn't stick, and after four
attempts, it opened a quarter inch, which was plenty of
room for the three nymphs to climb inside, find the paper,
stamps, pens, and envelopes, and carry them to the desktop.

Shiny and Impy worked on the letter. Impy thought Louis Armstrong would enjoy something written in a style that was formal and elaborate, whereas Shiny wanted to explain that Pops needed money and ask Louis Armstrong to come in the very first sentence. Demo favored brevity: *Pops, club, debt, help.* After much discussion, they agreed that Shiny would write the first two sentences and Impy the next two, including all of Demo's words. All three nymphs got underneath the pen to hold it up.

DEAR LOUIS ARMSTRONG,

AN OLD FRIEND OF YOURS, HERBERT WIGGINS, IS IN DEBT.

HIS JAZZ CLUB, POP'S CORNER, COULD BE FORECLOSED ON BY THE BANK IN FORTY-FOUR DAYS. PLEASE BE SO KIND AS TO CONSIDER COMING HERE FOR A BENEFIT PERFORMANCE TO HELP RAISE MONEY FOR THIS VITAL AND HISTORIC ENTERPRISE. THOUSANDS EAGERLY AWAIT YOUR KINDEST CONSIDERATION AND RESPONSE.

WITH WARMEST REGARDS,
FRIENDS OF POPS AND EARLENE

"Where does Louis Armstrong live?" Impy asked.

No one knew.

Finally Shiny said, "We can send the letter to the postal service. They'll track down Louis Armstrong, because they're proud of their work. They deliver the mail on time even when it's raining or snowing."

"How do we mail it?"

"We'll slide it under the door before the mailman comes. He'll see it on the step and pick it up."

They did this early the next morning, then watched from the windowsill. Sure enough, the mailman scooped up the letter and put it in his bag.

CHAPTER EIGHT

Waiting

IMPY, SHINY, AND DEMO were disappointed when no answer came the day after they sent the letter, or the next day, or the next.

"What in the world is wrong with Louis Armstrong?" Impy asked the others.

"Maybe he's so busy that he hasn't had a chance to write back," Shiny said. "Or maybe he lost his pen, or couldn't find a stamp."

Demo just stood there.

"We'll wait another day," Impy said. "If we don't hear from him by then, we'll have to make a backup plan."

* * *

A fourth day passed with no reply from Louis Armstrong. Impy was getting really nervous. "What's the matter with Louis Armstrong? Doesn't he care about his friends? Why hasn't he bothered to write back?"

"Shut up," Shiny said. She hummed "St. Louis Blues" and tapped the rhythm with her two front feet.

Demo just stood there.

"We have to make a contingency plan," Impy said.

"We will," Shiny agreed amiably. "But first I want to go upstairs and watch TV."

"This is more important than TV."

"Don't be a worrywart," Shiny said.

"I'm not!" Impy growled. He hated it when the other nymphs called him names.

"Sorry. How about just one show? Afterward we'll figure out your contin . . . whatever it's called."

Impy didn't agree, but he didn't want to be left out. He followed Shiny and Demo up the wall to the second floor. The TV was turned off. Earlene was in bed, talking on the telephone.

"That's wonderful! I can't wait to see it. . . .

"Ask your daddy to drop you by. He can bring Bitty too, if he wants. . . .

"No, I don't need to check with Herbert. This is one decision I can make on my own. . . .

"Let me talk to him."

You could tell from the change in tone that Earlene was now speaking to her son, Charlie, instead of her grandson.

"The children don't wear me out—I feel *better* when they come. . . .

". . . At eleven? Good. Send them straight upstairs."

"Hurray!" Shiny clapped her forelegs. "Troy and Bitty are coming at eleven!" The clock beside the bed said nine thirty.

"I'm going home." Impy was still mad. But Shiny didn't seem to notice.

"I wouldn't mind taking a nap," she said. "We were up most of the night, exploring the tiles behind the basement sink."

"Home." Demo nodded.

They scurried off, agreeing to meet behind Earlene's bureau at eleven o'clock.

CHAPTER NINE

Home, Sweet Home

IMPY'S HOME WAS A SMALL corner above the northeast ceiling tiles in the men's room of the bar. His mom had made it comfortable by providing tiny woven mats for her many children to sleep on. This morning, his mother embraced him with her forelegs. "I've been saving some special tidbits for us to eat together," she said. She brought out bits of a mushroom-and-cheese pizza she'd found in a discarded pizza box in the alley. She and Impy sang a little song before they ate. It was one Impy had created when he was very small:

"Sun and moon,
Snow and rain,
Dark and light,
And dark again."

Soon some of the other brothers and sisters came to join them. The food was broken into smaller bits and shared without complaint.

Impy had so many brothers and sisters that he could hardly keep them straight. There were Hera, and Eureka, and Plato, all fathered by the Socra line. Silvio and Encanta were descended from the more musical branch of the community. As far as Impy knew, he was the only one in the family who had a father from outside the jazz club. His mother rarely spoke about his dad, but when she did, her eyes shone and she murmured softly to Impy, "He was a very special roach. His shell was a dark, shiny chestnut color, and his legs and antennae were as black as night."

"What was his name?"

"Petronovich Roach. His heritage was Russian. He was a revolutionary who went from city to city, helping roaches in need. So I don't really expect to see him again."

"Petronovich," Impy repeated to himself like a mantra. "Petronovich."

CHAPTER TEN

๑๛

Troy Finds Out

THE CHILDREN ARRIVED right on time. Pops was glad to see his grandkids, of course, but he had so much on his mind, what with Earlene's illness and his money troubles, that he hardly had the energy to smile. So he kissed Troy and Bitty and sent them upstairs to be with their grandmother.

Their presence made her day. Lying in bed can be lonely, especially when you're not feeling well, and lately her husband had been so preoccupied that he hardly seemed to hear what she was saying.

The children were excited too. They brought their lunch boxes, a set of LEGOs, a deck of cards, and a large black box with a handle on top. This was carried carefully by Troy, while Bitty dumped the rest of the supplies onto the foot of the bed.

Troy approached, still carrying the box. Earlene realized suddenly what it was.

"Open it!" she cried.

"Let me!" Bitty squealed, but her grandma's arm held her in check while Troy unclasped the case and withdrew a big, shiny trumpet. Its glow seemed to light the entire bedroom.

"You finally got it!" Earlene's eyes were as bright as Troy's. "Have you had any lessons?"

"Only one." Troy looked embarrassed. "It's harder than it looks."

"Play me something."

"I want to show Grandpa, too."

Earlene nodded. "Then maybe we should wait until he's finished his work. What would you like to do till then?"

"Watch TV."

"Okay, Bitty, here's the remote. How about you, Troy?"

"I think I'll read."

"You can use Grandpa's easy chair. Or if the TV's too loud, you can go downstairs and sit in his office."

Troy loved Grandpa's office: the faded photographs and newspaper clippings on the walls, the smell of cigar smoke, the piles of records and CDs. He leaned back in the chair and put his feet up on the big old desk the way Pops did. Today his shoe dislodged a handful of papers. Troy bent and picked them up.

The letter on top caught his eye first: Internal Revenue Service, amount past due: $4000. Troy thought it must be a mistake. But under that was a statement from the bank—listing even bigger debts. The date in the corner of each letter was recent—only a few weeks ago! The bills added up to more than $11,000. Had Grandpa already paid the money? Where in the world could he have found that much?

This time Troy read the letters carefully. His alarm increased. Not only did Grandpa owe an enormous sum of money, but the bank was threatening to foreclose on the club, and the apartment too. Where could Grandma and Grandpa live without the apartment? Didn't the people in the bank know that Grandma was sick?

"And she doesn't know about this, either," Troy realized suddenly, whispering to himself. "She wouldn't be so cheerful if she did." He looked at Pops's calendar. The foreclosure date was only thirty-nine days away. He put his head between his hands and tried to think of what to do.

CHAPTER ELEVEN

The Trumpet

WHEN TROY WENT DOWNSTAIRS, Shiny decided to stay
in the bedroom and spy on Bitty. Impy and Demo agreed to
stay with her. They'd watched Troy a lot, because he was older
and had spent more time at the club; but it was only recently
that Bitty had been allowed to come for more than a brief
visit, "Because she can be difficult." The idea that a single
small human could create as much chaos as Bitty did seemed
amazing. She was like a stick of dynamite on legs.

This morning Bitty was in good form. She got bored
watching TV and decided to sing. Earlene, who was a tiny
bit deaf, didn't mind at all. At first she sang along with her

granddaughter: "Farmer in the Dell," "Old MacDonald had a Farm," "Baa, Baa, Black Sheep." But Bitty seemed to have interminable energy, and she proceeded to sing "Just a Closer Walk with Thee," "Jailhouse Rock," "The Star-Spangled Banner," "Love Potion No. 9," "Bop She Bop," and a sequence of other classics. Earlene listened in awe. Bitty's sense of rhythm and pitch was unerring. Demo and Shiny couldn't help tapping their feet. They started to sway and then to dance on the top of the bureau. They joined their top set of legs and spun and twirled to Bitty's music. Impy felt left out. He wondered what Troy was doing downstairs.

Bitty kept on singing. She outlasted Demo and Shiny, who finally dropped in exhaustion. Earlene leaned back against her pillow and started snoring. Impy felt like screaming: *What about Pops? What about the club? Why are we singing and dancing when our home and families are in danger?*

He reminded Shiny of that later. She was philosophical. "We should have fun while we can. If we ruin our time worrying, we might as well have left the club the minute we heard the news."

"That's ridiculous! If we can come up with a good enough plan, we won't have to move!"

"We did come up with a good plan," Shiny reminded Impy. "We wrote the letter, and we mailed it. Now we're waiting to hear back."

"But we haven't heard. So we need to make another plan, in case the first one doesn't work."

"Louis Armstrong will answer, even if he doesn't have

the money. Close as he and Pops were, he's bound to. Don't you remember how Pops talks about him?" Shiny's voice got dreamy. "Like he's the greatest man who ever lived. Almost beyond a man—like an angel!"

"You're probably right," Impy agreed. "But I still think—"

SCRREEEEEPP! The blast nearly knocked them off their feet. Demo leaped up, terrified. Earlene groaned in her sleep. Even Bitty stopped her song and stood stock-still, too amazed to utter a word.

Immediately there came another blast. Earlene woke up. "Did you hear something?" she asked. Bitty just stared at her. A third blast shook the walls and made Earlene cover her ears. "Lord in Heaven, call the police!" she said.

"Downstairs!" Shiny snapped. "As fast as you can move!"

The nymphs raced down the back of the bureau, around the corner, and through the crack in the apartment floor. In a moment they were huddled on the ceiling of the lounge.

What they saw was this: Pops standing in the doorway with Troy beside him. And in Troy's hands was the shiny gold trumpet.

"It can't be," Shiny whispered. "Because a trumpet makes *music*."

As if to rebut her, Troy raised the instrument to his lips. What came out sounded like a wreck between two speeding cars. Even Pops looked stunned. After a few seconds he managed a shaky smile.

"Want me to do it again?"

"Uhhhh . . . sure. But maybe we'd better step outside."

"Can't we go upstairs? Grandma wants to hear it too."

"Grandma might be sleeping now. Maybe you can play for her tomorrow, or the next day. When do you start your lessons?"

"I already had one, but that teacher said he wasn't a good match for me. So last night Dad found someone better. He's at the Peabody Conservatory."

"The conservatory . . . isn't that the fancy music school downtown?"

"Yes, he says they're the best."

"Ummm, maybe they can do something with you . . . I mean, they'll probably teach you a lot."

"Yes." Troy beamed. "I can't wait."

But later, helping Pops sweep the barroom floor, Troy was unusually quiet. Pops asked, "Cat got your tongue?"

"No, not really . . . but, Grandpa?"

"What?"

"If you had a problem, you could tell me about it."

Pops chuckled. "That's nice, son."

"I mean it, Grandpa.

You've helped me lots of times—like getting the trumpet. I know you talked to Daddy."

"Oh, well . . ." Pops didn't deny it.

"And I'd like to help you back."

"You help me just by being who you are."

Gruffly, Pops put his arm around Troy and kissed his head.

CHAPTER TWELVE

೧ஐ୬

The Response

IMPY WAITED FOR THE MAIL. Every day when papers started pouring through the slot, he scurried among the envelopes. Letters came from the bank, the state of Maryland, and the IRS, but there was nothing from Louis Armstrong. "Only thirty-six days till the foreclosure," he told the others. "Thirty-six days left, and we haven't heard a thing."

"Shut up, Imp." Even now, with more time passing, Shiny was not inclined to worry. She did a little dance. "The Socras are debating whether it's best to move on a Tuesday or a Wednesday," she said. "Once they decide, they'll send a mission to explore the outside world!" The nymphs had little concept of "the outside world," because they weren't allowed to leave the building. They did know there were other roach colonies besides their own. Most lived well and obeyed a code of ethics drawn up by the ancients. Others were rebels. One group, the Transients, were always on the move; another, the Creepies, hung out in gangs and lived outside the law. But most roach communities stayed in touch and tried to help each other out.

Shiny went on: "My cousins found out there's a new McDonald's on Loch Raven Road. They heard that the storeroom was wonderful, so they sent two explorers to check it out. When they got inside, they couldn't believe their eyes. The closet shelves were filled with *bug spray*."

"I hate the word *bug*! It's so demeaning."

"Socra-Roach says humans don't know better, because they're a new species. As they age, they'll get smarter."

"They claim that they invented the calendar."

Shiny remembered history class. "They copied it from roach tablets and pretended it was theirs."

"Same with the Greek philosophies?"

"Yes. One of them even took the master's name: Socrates."

"Haven't they come up with *anything* original?"

"The Pepsi-Cola jingle is theirs, and the Happy Birthday song. I like that one." Shiny did a little dance while she sang it. "*Happy birthday to you; happy birthday—*"

Crash! Today's mail came tumbling through the slot. Demo held the others back. Sometimes the postman saved the magazines till last, and if they hit you, you were roach jelly. Impy was dying to get into the pile. Finally Demo released them. Shiny started tunneling through the grocery-store circulars. Impy, crawling upside down across the face of the pile of letters, cried out, "It's come! It's finally come!"

And he read, slowly and proudly, the return address:

"Louis Armstrong Institute
132 Whitlow Street
Queens, New York."

The three friends chewed a hole in the top of the envelope. Then they pressed against the tear and made it longer. They slid the letter out and carried it into the coat closet. Impy stood in the center of the piece of paper and read triumphantly.

"Dear Friends of Pops and Earlene's:

Thank you for your interest in the late
Louis Armstrong.

How we wish he were available to
play a benefit for the jazz club
you describe in your letter. Many
historic institutions, both large and
small, deserve recognition as standard-
bearers for the development of forms of
American music, but instead, like
yours, they face
foreclosure and destruction at the
hands of those who value profit more
than our cultural heritage. . . ."

There was no money inside the envelope, and the letter didn't say when any would be sent. Even Shiny, usually so optimistic, felt depressed.

"Louis Armstrong certainly *is* late," she sighed. "If he doesn't hurry up, there's no telling what's going to happen."

She burst into tears.

Impy fought to keep his own tears back.

Demo just stood there.

CHAPTER THIRTEEN

The Elder Roach Council

IN THE MEANWHILE, all ideas for dealing with Pops's problems were being sent to the four highest roach officials, the highest of whom was Socra-Roach. Every day the Elder Roach Council—Socra-Roach, Carlita Banan, Felix Harlequin, and Meg Maddie—met to consider the proposals. Sometimes Impy hid in a hole in the ceiling overhead and listened to their conversation.

This morning's meeting began with tea and a reading from the ancient Greek poet Sappho-Roach.

"Oh, Sister Roaches,

Have courage, and fight against all obstacles!

Be warriors of the mind first,

Body, second!

Face the enemy with courage, determination,

And quick wit.

Let no one die!"

Then Socra-Roach asked Carlita to review the latest ideas. She picked up the tiny stack of papers in front of her. Her six feet shuffled in a muted Calypso beat.

"First, we have the Internet fund-raising efforts," she reported. "These will begin on Monday. The Web site for contributions will be www.savepops.com."

Socra-Roach adjusted a tiny pair of glasses. He waggled his walking stick at Felix.

"Any report from the Harlequins?"

Felix had a background in science theory. "We may sell one of our mathematical formulas to Princeton University. They can pretend it was developed by their own scientists, like they did with Albert . . . what was his last name again?"

"Einstein," Socra-Roach muttered. He slumped back on the end of his shell. "There's a problem with that. . . . Anyone?"

Meg Maddie hissed, "Didn't Albert allow his work to be used on the . . ."

"Atomic bomb. Exactly." Socra-Roach nodded. "So if you were to sell the humans a new formula, you'd have to consider the ramifications. We wouldn't want the knowledge used to hurt someone."

"How about the equation that tells what happens when you die? Or the thought-transfer?"

"That one needs a filter—remember how much trouble it caused us?"

There was a moment of silence. No one could forget the feud that had taken place when the Green Banans had intercepted a thought message from the Harlequins wishing for peace and quiet instead of twenty-four hours of polka. It had taken weeks to resolve the issue, and bad feelings still lingered. Carlita nodded. "They might end up getting mad at each other. We wouldn't want that."

Meg Maddie had a suggestion. "What about getting our own credit card and paying off the debts with that?"

"Eventually we'd have to pay the bill. When we defaulted, the foreclosure process would start all over again." Socra-Roach paced back and forth behind his desk. His tiny stick clacked on the wooden floor. "We have ninety-one dollars in our treasury. Two months ago we sent a check for four hundred dollars to the National Roach Medical Fund. Of course, back then we had no idea that we'd soon need cash ourselves."

"It's an awful lot of money," Carlita murmured. The other leaders nodded. The silence at the table was unusual.

After a while Meg Maddie cleared her throat. "Some of my family want to explore new sites," she confessed.

"You mean you Maddies are already bailing out?" Carlita's voice was sharp.

"You ought to turn down the music and face reality: we may have to leave here."

"Peace, sister roaches. The right solution is around

the corner. We just haven't recognized it yet."

"Felix is right—but so are both of you." Socra-Roach sighed. "We're *all* thinking about sending out scouts," he said. "And we should be. But I think that we should work together, instead of separately. We'll cover more ground and have more resources between the four families than any single group has on its own. . . ." He closed his eyes for a moment. "There's something else . . . I didn't mention it at the meeting because I thought it would add to the upset.

"After Pops left the bank with me in his jacket lining, he went straight to the hospital. The doctors told him that Earlene is very sick. Her heart is weak and getting weaker. She may live only a few more months. If she loses her home, think what that would do to the short time she has left."

CHAPTER FOURTEEN

ᘓᔍᕬ

Thirty-two Days Left, and Counting

IMPY THOUGHT OF A NEW PLAN. It was so scary that he didn't dare tell Shiny or Demo or Socra-Roach or even his own mother.

The idea came to him at night, while he lay on his reed mat next to his many brothers and sisters. He had been meditating—letting the slow relaxing rhythms of the mantra wash over him—when he began to hear a voice. It was whispering his name: "*Impetuous Roach . . . Impetuous Roach . . .*"

Nobody calls me that, he answered silently. *I'm Impy*. But when he ended the meditation, he began to ponder what he'd heard. Who, besides his mother, knew his proper name? Certainly none of the other nymphs. His mom had thought *Impetuous* was too long for a baby's name and had shortened it to Impy. The voice he'd heard had been male. Could it belong to his father? Maybe somehow he'd learned that Impy was in trouble. If that were true, Impy needed to let him know what the trouble was, and where, and what kind of help was needed. If a remarkable and heroic roach like Petronovich set himself to the task, surely Pop's Corner would be saved.

There were problems, of course. Petronovich traveled from city to city, so no one ever knew where he was. There were only thirty-two days till the foreclosure. Impy would have to figure out a way to spread the word as far and wide as possible. He sat on his bed and thought. In the darkness he got up, unpacked his school supplies, and found a pen and paper.

Impy printed in tiny script:

A message to my father, Petronovich,
Our home, Pop's Corner, will be foreclosed
on by a bank unless we raise $11,000.
More than 700 roaches—including me!—will
be homeless. Please help.
From your son, Impetuous Roach (Impy)

Under the message to his father, he added a note in larger letters:

ALL ROACHES TRAVELING TO THE EAST, WEST, NORTH,
AND SOUTH, PLEASE MEMORIZE THIS MESSAGE, SPREAD
IT TO EVERY ROACH YOU MEET, AND ASK THAT HE
OR SHE PASS IT ON, TOO. THANK YOU, I. R.

The problem, of course, was putting the notice where it would be seen.

CHAPTER FIFTEEN

Someone Knows

SHINY AND DEMO KNEW NOTHING of Impy's plan. They continued to spy on the children in Earlene's bedroom.

Bitty was in high spirits. "I want to sing with Grandma!" she demanded. But Earlene turned first to Troy.

"How did you like the teacher from the music school?" she asked.

Troy bit his lip. He didn't look as cheerful as Earlene might have expected. "He said he wasn't right for me," he murmured. "He's going to help us find someone else."

"Somebody else? Isn't that what the last one said?" Earlene was indignant for a second. But when she saw Troy starting to take the trumpet out of its case, she remembered the screeches that had wakened her last week and nodded slowly to herself. In the meantime, Bitty's arms and hands stretched toward the shiny gold instrument. It was almost as big as she was.

"No, Bitty, this trumpet is mine. You're too little to play music. And if you make a fuss, I'll put it away."

"I'm *not* too little! I'm big!"

Reluctantly, Troy nestled the horn back into the black velvet inside the case, then snapped it shut. He didn't notice the expression of relief that flitted over Earlene's face.

"*No* fair! It's my turn!"

"I've got a new video," Grandma intervened. "And I'm going to give Troy money to go to the corner store and buy us soda and potato chips."

"Soda! I want soda!"

Earlene gave Troy a five-dollar bill.

"You sure you want me to spend this, Grandma?"

"Of course. What better use for money than to have a picnic with my grandchildren?"

Troy swallowed. *He* could think of a better use, but he couldn't tell Grandma what it was.

Before he left, he set his trumpet in the coat closet in the front hall. It scrunched against a piece of trash. Troy picked it up to throw it out. The minute he saw the words *Louis Armstrong Institute*, he became curious. He read the letter once, then over again. His heart beat faster. He looked around the room. *Dear Friends of Pops and Earlene's . . .* What friends? he wondered. Could Grandpa have sent a letter asking for help? No, Pops would never use someone else's name. If he'd asked for something, which—given his pride—Troy doubted that he had, Grandpa would have signed the request himself.

But who else? Troy wondered. And why had he or she left the letter on the closet floor?

"No fair!" echoed faintly from upstairs. Troy remembered his errand and the five-dollar bill tucked in his pants pocket. He folded the letter carefully and put it in his pocket, too. His head swirling with questions, he headed down the street to the corner store.

CHAPTER SIXTEEN

ᲚᲚᲚ

To the Lamppost

IMPY THOUGHT about how to get the message for his father to a place where other travelers would see it. He decided to hike to the busy intersection two blocks north of the club and fasten the notice to a lamppost there.

Why didn't he tell Socra-Roach and ask the elder to send somebody older and more streetwise in his place? The truth was he feared that Socra-Roach wouldn't think his father could solve the problem. Impy knew what an incredibly powerful and intelligent roach Petronovich was, but Socra-Roach might not. Instead he might think, What kind of father would have a son and walk away, leaving him with nothing but a name?

He could have asked Shiny and Demo to go with him. But then there would be three nymphs breaking the rules instead of one. Not only that, but Shiny might dance down the sidewalk, forgetting to watch out for people's feet. Demo might get separated from the others and panic. No, it was best for Impy to go alone.

The journey would not be safe. Creepies hung out in groups on some of the corners, slouching against the walls of the closest buildings. They wore little hats pulled low over their heads, and they made a habit of hassling or sometimes even robbing other roaches. All the nymphs knew about the Creepies because of the rhyme the older nymphs repeated to the young ones:

> *The Creepies are a'comin',*
> *And they're a'comin' fast.*
> *If you see them on your sidewalk,*
> *You'd better let them pass.*
> *They'll kick you in the morning,*
> *They'll crack your joints at night.*
> *For there's nothing that the Creepies*
> *Like better than a fight.*
>
> *They'll curse your name at daybreak,*
> *They'll slap you during lunch.*
> *They'll steal your sister's candy*
> *And laugh to hear it crunch.*
> *They'll act like you can have some,*
> *Then swallow every bite.*
> *For there's nothing that the Creepies*
> *Like better than a fight.*

When Socra-Roach heard the rhyme, he told the nymphs to stop. "They're not as bad as you think," he said. "Their elders make them give back whatever they've stolen, and if they curse, they have to clean their corner for the next two weeks."

The nymphs would pipe down then, but as soon as Socra-Roach and the other adults left, they'd start chanting the rhyme all over again.

Impy shivered. No matter what Socra-Roach said about the Creepies, Impy hoped against hope that he wouldn't run into them.

He was afraid, but he made a detailed plan and stuck to it. He climbed up to the windowsill at six that morning, when he knew most roaches were asleep. His poster was rolled into a tube, with bits of paste stuck to all four corners. Holding his breath, Impy scrambled through the jagged screen and started down the outside wall.

Socra-Roaches have exceptional navigational instincts, because in the far, far past, many of them had traveled the rough Aegean Sea. The Green Banans built rafts and sailed from island to island in the South Atlantic, mapping their journeys as they went. But Impy was neither Socra nor Banan, and when he reached the bottom of the wall he had no idea which way to turn. What direction was north? *V-roooom, v-roooom!* Huge cars passed somewhere in the distance. Trying not to panic, Impy searched for the sun: there it was, just off the horizon. So that must be east, and the opposite direction, west. That means north would be . . . where all the racket was coming from. Well, if he wanted to put the notice where everyone would see it, he'd have to head that way, no matter how noisy it was. How far was the intersection? Impy wasn't sure. He ran as fast as he could, staying on the edge of the sidewalk. But the poster was heavy, and several times he had to stop and rest.

The noise was growing louder. Far ahead, Impy could see cars, trucks, and buses passing on a street that ran perpendicular to the one where he was now. Beside the busy thoroughfare, humans moved along the sidewalks. Their shoes smashed down with no regard for whatever might lie beneath them. They walked under a green metal structure with a glass globe on top of it. Impy drew closer. His own street seemed abandoned; not a single insect passed him on the sidewalk. He looked again at the tall green tower up ahead and realized it must be the lamppost. He was not so very far away when reality hit him like an arrow in the chest. To reach the lamppost he would have to cross the busy sidewalk in front of it.

I should go back, Impy thought. I broke the rules to come here anyway.

I should go back, Impy thought. If I get hurt, my mother will be very sad.

I should go back, Impy thought. No one will know that I have failed.

Except me.

CHAPTER SEVENTEEN

Roach Rules

"HAVE YOU SEEN IMPY?" Shiny asked. The other nymphs were on their way to practice kick-the-crumb.

"You mean that runty little mutt you hang out with?"

"Shut up, Freddie—that's not funny! I'm worried about him. I've been looking everywhere."

"Ask the giant birdbrain. Isn't he your best friend too?"

"I'm going to tell Carlita what you said." Shiny was furious. "You're breaking the rules. She can throw you out of the tournament, you know."

"I'm so-o-o-o-o sorry." Freddie had always been a

jerk. He bounced the crumb with his front leg, passed it to his hind one, then bounced it forward again. "See you later, Shiny."

Demo hadn't seen Impy either. He'd been busy fetching water for the Socra elders, who were lying on tiny couches and discussing—endlessly—the topic of location, and whether or not it had an influence on one's thinking. Demo listened while he poured the water into tiny bowls.

When the first group argued that location and evolution went hand in hand, he tended to agree with them; but when the others answered that who you are is formed by your character, not your environment, he thought they might be right, too. Then Shiny was pulling at his foreleg, whispering, "Have you seen Impy?"

Demo shook his head.

"We should look for him," Shiny went on.

Demo checked the water bowls. Every single one was filled. He followed Shiny.

They didn't have to look far. Just as they came around the corner near the bathroom ceiling tiles, Impy appeared in front of them.

"Where have you been?" Shiny started twirling her antennae ribbons. "I was worried—"

"I slept late."

"Your mat was empty."

"That's 'cause I fell asleep inside the crack next to the storage room."

Shiny frowned at him. "We never go there."

"I know, only—"

"Impy! What happened to your feet?"

Impy looked down. Little trails of blood marked the place where he'd been standing.

"How did you hurt yourself? Where in the world have you been?"

The rules of the roach communities that lived at Pops's were spelled out clearly:

1. *Aid other roaches when they need your help*
2. *Be courteous to all*
3. *Set a good example for the nymphs*
4. *Stereotyping: statements such as "All Socras are eggheads," or "All Green Banan roaches are musicians," is not permitted*
5. *Nymphs are not allowed outside the premises without express permission and adult supervision*
6. *No nymphs allowed in Pops and Earlene's apartment*

There were myths that illustrated what could happen if roaches broke the rules. One of Impy's favorites was the tale of Foodle, an arrogant nymph who neglected to help an elderly roach who had hurt his foreleg in an accident. Despite the wounded roach's cries, Foodle had run right past and helped himself to a chunk of leftover pasta on the kitchen floor. Seconds later, an enormous wall of straw had descended and swept Foodle into a black metal tray filled with dust and dirt. Before he could scream, he was tossed into a dark space. The steep walls were made of slippery plastic. Foodle began to howl, but there was no one who could hear him—except, perhaps, the wounded roach whose cries he had ignored. How surprised he was when, later, rappeling down the wall, came a brigade of roach emergency workers. They slipped him into a vest knotted with thin string, then gave a yank. Foodle felt himself lifted carefully, inch by inch, up the dark wall. A crack opened in the plastic, and he was pulled through, into the light. When he looked around, he saw the elderly roach, with a bandage on his leg. "You . . . you told them?" The old one nodded.

Foodle bowed down so low his antennae scraped the floor. The elder accepted Foodle's apology, but Foodle was so embarrassed by his behavior that he left his clan and traveled all the way to Asia in a shipping container. He was never heard from again.

The ending of the story sent shivers down Impy's exoskeleton. He and Shiny and Demo had broken rule number six many times, but they'd never been found out. But what if someone from the club happened to travel to the intersection? What if he or she saw the notice on the lamppost and told Socra-Roach about it? What would happen to Impy then?

I should have thought about the consequences of my actions, Impy realized. On the other hand, maybe Petronovich would come, like a roach in shining armor. He'd have a check for $11,000 folded in his saddlebag. When he saw Impy, he'd swoop down and pull him up onto the saddle in front of him, and they'd ride like heroes through the admiring hordes.

CHAPTER EIGHTEEN

Twenty-eight Days Left, and Counting . . .

TROY BROKE THE RULES, TOO. When his dad poked his head into Troy's bedroom before breakfast, Troy said he was sick. He almost never lied to his father; in fact, he hated lying. But today he wanted to stay home by himself. He had a plan, and he could only do it alone.

His father never doubted what Troy said. He brought him ginger ale and ice and said he'd call at noon to see how he was feeling. But after the front door slammed and the car pulled out of the driveway, Troy got up. He put on his church clothes: a dark suit, blue shirt, red necktie, and leather shoes. He stood before the mirror to make sure he looked okay. Then he drank a glass of orange juice and brushed his teeth. He took some money and a folded piece of paper from his bedside table, put them in his pocket, walked outside, and locked the door behind him.

Troy caught the bus at St. Charles and Fifteenth, headed downtown. He watched the numbers on the buildings: 1300, 1205, 1117, 1004. When the bus moved onto the 900 block, Troy pulled the cord and got off. He looked at the large granite building to his left, swallowed, and went inside.

He had never seen the bank's headquarters. The building had marble columns, marble floors, massive windows, and a ceiling so high you could almost have fit a house inside the room. The big wooden counters and tables made Troy feel very small. He wasn't sure which way to turn. A security guard, a young woman with curly red hair, must have noticed his confusion. "Are you in the right place?" she asked gently.

Troy nodded. "I need to see Samuel Shaw." That was the signature on the letter he had seen on Grandpa's desk.

The guard looked vaguely amused. "Samuel Shaw is the president of the bank," she said.

Troy nodded. That made sense. "Where is his office?"

The guard stared at him for a moment, then decided to take his request seriously. "His office is in Chicago, at the bank headquarters."

"But I thought this—"

"This is the *local* headquarters. Our manager is Thomas Foley."

"Oh." Troy was confused. Would Mr. Foley know

about the letter? He swallowed again. "I'd like to see him, then."

"You can't without an appointment."

"Where do I make an appointment?" Troy could be stubborn, and when he felt someone was trying to thwart him, that made him more stubborn still.

"I guess you could speak with his secretary. . . ." The guard seemed puzzled by Troy's perseverance. "What's this about?"

"Bank business. My grandfather has an account here."

"Why didn't he come himself?"

"Could I please speak to Mr. Foley's secretary?"

"Second door to the left—office number one."

The secretary wasn't helpful, either. When Troy came in she smiled and took a piece of candy out of a metal dish on her desk. "Looking for this?"

"No, I need to make an appointment with Mr. Foley. I have to talk to him about a bank account."

"Your account?"

"No, my grandfather's."

The secretary was about to say no, when a tall, balding man came rushing in, headed for the door behind the secretary's desk. When he saw Troy, he stopped short, and his worried look changed to a smile. "Why, who's this?"

"He came in saying he wanted an appointment with you—something about his grandfather's account. I was just about to tell him—"

But Mr. Foley had heard enough. "Come in, young man," he boomed in a voice much bigger than his narrow frame. He opened his office door. "Come right in."

* * *

Mr. Foley knew about Pops's problems. "I put off action for as long as I could," he told Troy sadly. "But the directors in Chicago haven't met your granddad. I told them about the club—I went there as a boy, with my parents, so I remember it well—but they say business isn't based on feelings. To make matters worse, they've already found a buyer for the building."

"Did you know that my grandma is sick?" Troy asked.

"I didn't know that. Mr. Wiggins just said that he would find the money somewhere. But he's said that for so long . . ." Mr. Foley sighed. "I like your grandfather," he said. "He's a good person, and he's given lots of young musicians a head start on their careers. He showcased talent that no one else would touch—until they got popular, that is. I wish there were something I could do for him."

"Other people are trying to help too." Troy unfolded the letter from his pocket. "I found this last week," he said.

Mr. Foley read the letter quickly. The frown lines in his forehead grew even more pronounced. He turned the paper over to see if anything was written on the back.

"This is very strange . . . Louis Armstrong has been dead for years. Certainly your granddad knows that. But whoever wrote the letter of inquiry obviously didn't." Mr. Foley stared at Troy gravely.

"You're sure you didn't write this yourself, Troy, to try and help your grandfather?"

"I didn't know there *was* a Louis Armstrong Institute," Troy answered. "And if I had, I wouldn't have thought to write to them."

Mr. Foley looked at Troy a second longer. Then he nodded, satisfied that Troy was telling the truth.

"I'm sorry," he said. "I wish there were something I could do." He stood up from his desk.

Troy got up too. He felt weak. "Could you please not tell my granddad I was here?"

"Of course I won't. And if you have a brainstorm, let me know." Mr. Foley nodded toward the reception area. "Miss Franklin guards the door, so here's my card. My private line is this one. . . ." He circled one of the numbers on the bottom.

"Thanks." Troy's shoulders slumped.

On the bus ride back, he felt depressed. At home, practicing his trumpet, he pretended to be Louis Armstrong. Then he noticed the next-door neighbor closing her windows. He put the trumpet away, changed his clothes, and walked down to the park with his soccer ball to practice dribbling.

CHAPTER NINETEEN

The Transients

THE POSTER ON THE LAMPPOST near Pop's Corner attracted more attention than Impy had imagined. The spot was a popular transfer station among Transient roaches: they could hop a ride east or west when a driver rushed into the nearby deli for a Coke or a pack of chips. They could drop through the sidewalk vents and land on top of the subway, which went to the train station. Or they could take a city bus (hopping on someone's shoe just before he or she got on) and descend (on another shoe) at the Greyhound station. Long-distance roach travelers tended to prefer the bus to the train, because the bus company's ideas about cleanliness was more lax and generally didn't include bug spray.

Among the roaches who noticed the poster were three friends who weren't headed to any particular destination. But they sought adventure, and having a mission appealed to them. When they discovered that each was inspired by the idea of finding Petronovich, they decided to split up and search in different directions. One would take the bus that traveled up the northeast corridor, stopping in Philadelphia, New York, and Boston. The second would head south, toward Atlanta and Miami. The third would go due west, toward Cleveland, Chicago, and finally California.

Of course they had their doubts. "We don't even know if he's alive," the first traveler pointed out. "And how will we signal each other if we find him?"

"Just put a notice at the bottom of the snack counter at the closest bus station, asking other Transients to spread the word. We'll hear soon enough. You know how roaches love gossip."

"Petronovich Roach . . . Very odd name, don't you think, mate?"

"Perhaps he's of Russian descent."

"What about *Impy*?"

"Who knows? Perhaps a mistake by the Maddies? They are rather easily . . . distracted, if you get my gist."

The third roach was younger and more tolerant. "Why, my cousin Otto is a hisser, and you never met a nicer roach."

"Nice, perhaps, but under the hat?"

"He never wore a hat." The young one knew exactly how the insult was intended. "They may start off more slowly than the rest of us, but once they hit their stride, they're awesome. Otto sat in on advanced math course at Harvard. He said it was laughably easy."

"Oh, my . . ." The first roach realized he had been reproached. "I didn't mean to suggest that they were—"

"Stupid? Far from it. The Maddies are just late bloomers."

The number seven bus arrived, headed directly to the Greyhound station. The three travelers each picked out a shoe and hopped on board. They knew they might not see each other again in the vast bus station.

"Cheers, mate!"

"Bye-bye!"

"Until we find Petronovich, and meet again."

༄

CHAPTER TWENTY

Impy Meets the Elder Roach Council

A FEW DAYS AFTER HIS TRIP to the lamppost, Impy was summoned to the Elder Roach Council. He hoped that they were calling him for an interview. Everyone knew that the council was getting ready to choose a group of explorers who would be sent away to search for home sites for the colony. Notices had been put up on every floor:

STRONG, QUICK-THINKING ROACHES

NEEDED IMMEDIATELY FOR

EXTREMELY DANGEROUS MISSIONS

Impy had thought that one would apply for these positions, rather than be summoned for an interview; his chest puffed out when he imagined the conversation as the council met: *Don't forget about the brilliant short nymph . . . What's his name again? Impy? We must certainly ask him if he's willing to participate.* Unfortunately, that wasn't exactly how the interview went.

When Impy came into the meeting, the first thing he saw were two strangers. One was slouched against the wall, a black hat pulled low over his forehead. The other had a leg band that read *RPU*. Each stranger took a look at Impy. The one with the hat spoke first:

"Him's the kid, all right. He hopped on our corner without asking, and I almost told my boys to jack him up and take him out. Then we seen he weren't nothin' but a little baby bugger."

Impy bristled. "I am not a baby!"

Socra-Roach silenced Impy and addressed the stranger. "Thank you."

The Creepie shrugged. "Just don't forget your dues to the big boss, Socra-dude. If you don't pay, we'll have to mess you up."

"I will gladly pay my dues as long as the money is returned to me the following day."

"You know we always gives it back! We ain't no double-dealers!" The Creepie swaggered off.

Now Socra-Roach turned to the roach with the RPU leg band. "Do you recognize this nymph?"

"I certainly do. He's the one I saw running down the avenue at seven o'clock on Monday morning. I made a report to my squad chief, because I knew the little fellow shouldn't be there."

"Thank you. We all appreciate the work of the patrol

units." Socra-Roach had the council clerk escort the stranger to the outside door.

When he turned back to Impy, he wasn't so polite. "What were you doing outside the building on Monday?" he demanded.

"Uhhh . . ."

"Don't bother to deny it. The Creepies saw you on their corner, and the Roach Patrol Unit spotted you near Harford Road. They followed you back here, to make sure you made it safe and sound."

"I . . . I needed some fresh air."

"Fresh air?"

"Ummm . . ." Impy tried a different tack. "I was curious. Everybody talks about outside, and I wanted to see it for myself."

"Did you ask permission?"

"Uhhhh . . ."

"Did you take someone with you?"

"I . . . uh . . ." Impy shuffled his six legs. "I didn't want anyone to know," he murmured.

"They said your feet were bleeding."

"I scratched them on the sidewalk. They're fine now." Impy showed Socra-Roach, who glanced at Impy's feet, then shook his head in irritation.

"Do you know what could have happened to you?"

"I was careful . . ."

"You broke the rules."

The members of the Elder Roach Council looked at each other and scratched their heads. Rule-breaking was uncommon. Socra-Roach was furious. "This is no time for disobedience. You could have been badly hurt, or even killed."

"I'm sorry."

"Quite appropriately so." Socra-Roach waggled his walking stick. "But sorry isn't sufficient. For the next month, I'm going to place you in the nursery with the babies. You'll be supervised full-time, to keep you out of trouble. You will help Bonita with the infants. Some of her assistants will be leaving on the exploratory missions, so she'll need some extra pairs of legs."

Impy wished that he could disappear.

A young council clerk walked Impy to the nursery. He had no idea what had happened in the meeting, and he asked too many questions: "Do you have new babies in the family? What are their names? Are you going to take them for a walk, or teach them how to read?"

Impy was silent. He could hear his feet making tiny clicks on the linoleum floor.

"What's wrong with you?" the clerk went on. "Did your best friend just check into a roach motel?"

Impy was sick of that stupid joke. He stared straight ahead and marched through the nursery door without looking back.

∞

CHAPTER TWENTY-ONE

The Envelope

"ARE YOU SURE there's nothing bothering you?" Earlene asked Pops the next morning as he was getting dressed. "You seem so quiet lately."

"Umph . . . just 'cause I'm quiet doesn't mean I'm bothered." Pops turned his back as he tucked in his shirt. He didn't want Earlene to see his expression.

"Maybe not, but it's just not like you. I'm afraid you're worried about me."

"Why do you say that?" Pops's tone was gruff.

"I just thought you might be, and if you are, I wanted to say this: Herbert, I know I won't live forever.

All that I ask is that I be allowed to stay here, in my own bed, with my family around me, for as long as possible."

Pops busied himself putting on his shoes. "Don't talk that way, honey."

"No, I'd rather be honest. That way we can make plans."

"Can't we talk about this some other time?"

"When?"

"Maybe tomorrow," Pops said. He couldn't look his wife in the face so he got up and went into the kitchen to make coffee and boil some eggs.

The day had begun badly and would only get worse. Pops could not bear to think that Earlene's one request—that she be at home with her family in her last days—might not be satisfied. Today was the day he had told the bank officer he would try to make a payment. He had managed to save a little from the performances of the previous week, but not nearly what was needed. And last night a fuse had blown on his big amplifier. He didn't have another, and the dead one would have to be replaced before tomorrow night's show.

Pops took his second cup of coffee into his office. There on the desk was the disaster all laid out: overdue payments, taxes, letters from banks he'd tried to borrow from to pay off everything else. There was even a note from a prospective buyer, asking to walk through the building so he could make plans. Pops tore it to shreds and threw it into the wastebasket. But then his anger turned to desperation. How could he break the news to

Earlene? He didn't think he had ever felt this bad in his life. He sat with his head in his hands, trying not to think of anything.

Pops was at the front door, ready to go out, when the mail came. He picked it up and glanced through the letters. There was a business envelope from Philadelphia. Did he owe money to someone there? Sighing, Pops ripped it open. Inside were ten twenty-dollar bills. He stared at them, then looked for a note. There was none.

He picked the envelope back up off the floor and looked at the return address: *BPOR, 33 HanfoRd StReet, Philadelphia, Pennsylvania*

He looked inside the envelope again: nothing. He checked his own address: *Pop's Corner, 116 Washington Street, Baltimore, Maryland.* There was no question; the envelope had been addressed to him.

Had he loaned somebody cash and forgotten about it? Was this the payback? If it was, he couldn't remember who it could be from. And why hadn't they sent a note?

Most likely it was a mistake. "Crazy," Pops muttered. He stuck the letter in his pocket.

At lunch he showed it to Earlene. She was as puzzled as he was. She looked at the return address, but it meant nothing to her.

"Maybe you should show it to George," she suggested. George was the mailman. He knew everybody's business and liked to talk about it. Pops wasn't sure about that.

"Tell George not to mention it to anyone," she added.

"To George that means tell *half* the people instead of every one of them."

Earlene smiled and didn't answer. But a little while later, when she was almost done with her soup, she said, "My daddy's friend belonged to a club that had nearly those initials. The members met in a brick building down near the courthouse. It was called the Elks Club, but the full name was the Benevolent and Protective Order of Elks."

"But this is different," Pops said. "It's BPO*R*."

"BPO*R*," Earlene murmured. Her eyes were starting to drift shut. "What in the world could that stand for?"

Pops didn't know. When he went back downstairs, he stuck the envelope, cash and all, in the top right-hand drawer of his desk. If someone had sent the money by mistake, it was certain they'd come back to claim it, and Pops didn't want to be accused of stealing. He was in bad enough trouble as it was.

CHAPTER TWENTY-TWO

The Nursery

BONITA, THE HEAD NURSE, made Impy's duties in the nursery absolutely clear. He was in charge of three newborns: Alicia, Peewee, and Horace. His job was to feed them, change their blankets, sing to them, and read them stories. Impy did this mindlessly because he was disgusted with himself. How could he have gone outside and up the block without thinking he'd be seen? Now he'd be stuck in the nursery while other roaches went out into the world, searching for homesites. If he hadn't been so stupid, mightn't he have been chosen to go with them?

He would never know. He spooned mashed crumbs

into the babies' mouths, changed them, read *The Little Red Nymph* and *The Pokey Little Roach* to them six times. After that, one of them began to cry.

He told Bonita.

"Which one?" she asked.

Impy shrugged. The truth was, he had tried to avoid looking at them because their mouths were covered with bread crumbs.

The nurse didn't like his answer. "Come with me," she ordered. Then she pointed out the difference between boy babies and girl babies.

Impy was embarrassed. "I *know* that already," he said.

"Then you should have guessed that this is Alicia. And between the boys, Peewee's shell is paler, and Horace has smaller antennae."

"Oh."

"It's very important to call each nymph by his or her name. We want each one to feel special."

Impy nodded. He'd never been especially fond of babies.

"Horace looks upset. Maybe he's the one who was crying. Here, pick him up—like this—and cuddle him. Then you can sing to him."

"Sing? I'm not a Green Banan, you know."

"Stereotyping is against the rules. Anyway, Harlequins sing too." Bonita sang quietly: *"Go to sleep, my little nymphie. Close your eyes and go to sleep . . ."* She rocked the baby for a minute, then handed the small bundle to Impy. "Here, you try it."

"Go to sleep, my smelly Horace. Shut your mouth or else I'll leave . . ." Impy realized suddenly that he'd said his thoughts out loud.

Bonita looked very annoyed. "I'm not leaving till you get it right," she said.

"*Go to sleep, my little Horace, so that I can . . .*" Impy couldn't remember the rest. Not only that, but there was a wet spot on his two front legs where Horace had been lying. "Yuck!" he said. "Here, take him back."

Bonita wouldn't. "You know how to change him," she said tartly.

"Do I have to?"

She didn't bother to answer. Impy had the feeling that his work in the nursery was going to be very hard.

CHAPTER TWENTY-THREE

૭ೞಿ

The Missions

STRONG, QUICK-THINKING ROACHES
NEEDED IMMEDIATELY FOR
EXTREMELY DANGEROUS MISSIONS

WHILE IMPY FRETTED in the nursery, preparations for the missions were proceeding quickly. Many roaches, male and female, young and old, signed up for interviews. Finally the list of those who had been chosen was posted on the Elder Roach Council's door. Impy ran to look, hoping against hope that he'd been picked. "'Darkeye, Hissing Harry, Achilles, Tommy T . . .'" Impy read out loud. Finally he came to the bottom of the list. He started at the top again and read more carefully. When he'd gone through every single name again, he had to face the truth: he had not been chosen. The one thing that made him feel a little better—and he knew the thought was shameful—was that neither Demo nor Shiny was on the list, either.

The next day the colony held a party for the explorers in Pops's basement. Hundreds of roaches showed up, clinging to the cement walls, floors, and even the joists that held the first floor of the club in place. Socra-Roach spoke at length about the difficulty of the missions and the self-sacrifice required to make them. The council had interviewed candidates from all four branches of the colony, he went on. The selection process had been difficult. He was confident that they had chosen well. The explorers, outfitted with tiny backpacks, stood modestly when their names were called, and the rest applauded them. Then they filed out, headed far and wide. Impy ran after them.

"Take me too," he begged. "I'm small, and I can fit in places where you can't." The roach explorers turned and stared at him.

"I'll just go tell my mom," Impy hurried on. "And I'll pack a couple of things—my mat, and some string, and a pencil. I even have some bread crumbs I've been saving. . . ."

No one answered. The other roaches went on by. A Harlequin leader, his pack slung casually over one shoulder, stopped and patted Impy on the back. "Have patience, little brother," he whispered. "Life will unfold just as it should."

CHAPTER TWENTY-FOUR

Miss Adventure

SHINY WASN'T CHOSEN to go on the missions, either. She *should* have been, she knew, because her family was descended from generations of explorers. Not only that, but she herself had many special talents: dancing, singing, climbing, and fashion design. She chose all her own antennae ribbons, debating the virtues of each color or print; and some days she chose for her girl cousins, too. Their mothers always told Shiny how nice the youngsters looked.

She went to talk with Socra-Roach. "Why wasn't my name on the list?" she demanded.

"We need you here. We have to keep up standards while the

others are away. Just this morning I couldn't decide between my white toga and my black one. I almost called you to help me make the choice."

"Why didn't you?"

"It turned out the white one had a spot on it—some ketchup, actually."

"The black looks better on you anyway." Shiny eyed Socra-Roach carefully, to make sure she was right. Yes, his walking stick was black, so his toga ought to match it. But her mouth trembled. "It's boring to stay here."

"Not everyone can go."

"I'm special!"

Socra-Roach sighed. "The decision has been made," he said firmly. "I'm not going to change my mind."

Instead of dancing, Shiny stomped out of the elder's office, her pink antennae ribbons bouncing on her shoulders.

"I'm going anyway," she told Impy the next afternoon. "I don't care *what* Socra-Roach says."

"The explorers already left!"

"I'm going on my own."

"Where?"

It was clear that Shiny didn't know. "Somewhere exciting and beautiful and fun."

"You'll get caught. Then you'll be in trouble and have to work in the nursery, like me."

"Shut up, Imp. You have no idea what I'm planning to do."

* * *

Shiny thought about her personal expedition. She thought about it as she cleaned the family sleeping quarters, danced the fox-trot, recited the multiplication tables up to twenty, practiced signing her name with curlicues and a heart-shaped dot over the *i*: Shinola Banan.

The signature was nice, she thought, but it was missing something. Shiny remembered her great-great grandfather, who used to tell her tales about exploring the Blue Moccoco River. "Adventure is in our blood," he used to say. She wrote her name again, slowly and beautifully, this time using a pink pen to add the title

Miss Adventure.

She read it out loud. Cool! The next step was to figure out where the adventure would take place.

Shiny imagined herself searching for homes in Hollywood or New York City. A movie star's mansion might be suitable, or perhaps a yacht. She imagined her glorious return to Pop's, and the speech she'd give standing at the podium behind the refrigerator. How the others would applaud when she explained where they were moving . . . Maybe she could find a place for Pops and Earlene, too. Thinking about them, an idea fluttered like a butterfly into her mind. The more she studied the idea, the more she liked it. She would do what other roaches hadn't dared to: get human help. And the person she would get it from was Bitty.

The idea made perfect sense. They had a lot in common: they were young and beautiful, and they loved to sing and dance. They both got what they wanted by being brave and forceful. Shiny was so excited that she did a little jig.

Should she tell Impy about her plan? He might be jealous if she did, and he would certainly want to come. Then she would have to share the glory of her triumphs. No, she decided. Instead she would tell him the minute she got back. In the meantime she would leave him a note, so he wouldn't worry. She wrote it carefully:

Impy,
Gone on mission, Back soon,
Your best friend,
Shinola Banan, Miss Adventure

p.s. Shut up, Imp.

She hid the scrap of paper in her school supplies. She'd stick it in Impy's bedroll right before she left. She climbed the wall to the apartment, her small heart pounding with excitement. The grandkids were supposed to come this very morning.

᠎⟋᠎

CHAPTER TWENTY-FIVE

More Letters

BUT THAT DAY Troy came alone, because Bitty had a cold. He entered quietly; Pops was bent over a speaker. "Darn thing isn't working right," he growled. "Seems like I fixed it yesterday."

"I had another lesson, Gramps," Troy said, hoping the news would cheer Pops up.

"Who's your teacher now?"

"Susan. She's in the high school band. She can play three instruments."

Pops thought that was a bit of a comedown, compared to the famous Peabody Conservatory, but of course he didn't say so.

"When I played for her, she laughed and said I sounded like a train wreck."

"Did she show you how to do better?"

"Not really. She thinks I ought to try the flute."

"The flute? No jazz great ever played the flute!"

Troy shrugged. "She was nice. And she wants to keep me as her student, too."

Pops wasn't optimistic about the new teacher, but he kept that to himself. "I got a new group coming in tonight," he told Troy. "They're called the KitKats."

"Wish I could come." Troy wasn't allowed inside the club when it was open, because Pops served beer.

"I'll tell you what they're like. In the meantime, I'd better get this fixed. Why don't you go upstairs? Grandma's waiting for you there."

After Troy left, Pops slumped at one of the tables. He knew the wiring for the speaker would cost thirty dollars. Early that same morning he'd gone back to the bank. The manager, Mr. Foley, had been especially nice. "How's your wife doing? And your grandkids?"

Pops frowned. He couldn't ever remember talking to Mr. Foley about Chester, Troy, or Bitty. "Uhhh . . . okay, I guess. I mean, they're fine."

"Good. And if you think of anything I can do to help you personally, please let me know."

Find me several thousand dollars, Pops thought. But he shook hands with Mr. Foley anyway. He was a good person, and he wanted to help. The problem was, there was nothing he could do.

* * *

The new band created a stir. Their music turned out to be a combination of hip-hop and jazz. Their rhythms were complex and beautiful. Even so, Pops was astounded to read a rave review of their performance in the next day's *City Paper*. The description of the club wasn't as favorable:

Pop's Corner has excellent acoustics, but the stage is rickety, and the tables and chairs old and dilapidated. There is no service staff; drinks are served by the club's owner, Herbert Wiggins, better known as "Pops," whose vintage is as old as the club's. That can mean a long wait for a bottle of beer. Perhaps next time the KitKats will find a more comfortable venue in which to perform.

Pops was furious. He showed the article to Earlene, who tried to cheer him up: "Herbert, you're in the paper! If you hadn't let that band open here, they'd still be practicing in someone's basement."

"I'm not slow," Pops growled. "And that stage is as good as new."

"I'm proud of you." Earlene took Pops's hand in hers. "You gave those youngsters a chance to show what they could do."

That afternoon, when Earlene was asleep, Pops got out his toolbox. He screwed some metal braces into the stage, to make the corners tighter and stronger. Then he walked to the middle of the wooden platform, bent his knees, and bounced. The old stage creaked and groaned. Pops wasn't sure his repair had done much good. He checked the two-by-fours that supported the plywood surface. Maybe there were a couple of cracks, but nothing that was going to break in the next few weeks. Pops looked at the tables and chairs. He could remember the day he'd bought them as clearly as if it were last week. He'd ordered them from Baltimore Restaurant Supply, and they'd arrived in a huge delivery truck. They'd smelled like varnish and fresh wood. When he and Charlie had arranged them on the club floor, Pops's chest had swelled with pride. Charlie had been eight or nine. How old was he now? Forty-one? Or was it forty-two? Thirty-four years wasn't that old for furniture, was it? He let his gnarled hand run over one of the scratched, sticky tabletops. Maybe it *could* use a little sanding and a coat of paint, he told himself. When I get some extra money, that's the first thing I'll do. He tried to ignore the more realistic voice that whispered, *Unless you get a lot of extra money, three weeks from now you won't be standing in this club at all.*

Pops had put off sorting the mail because he knew it might contain another notice from the bank. Instead there were circulars and coupons for the local grocery store. Under those were two letters, both addressed by computers, so Pops assumed that they were junk and almost threw them out. But something stopped him. With his hands poised just above the trash can, he ripped the first one open and dumped out the contents. To his amazement, money floated through the air. Drawing in his breath, Pops grabbed. There were ten pieces of paper, each one a hundred-dollar bill. Pops gathered them up. He sat down on the floor, leaned his back against the wall, and took a deep breath. He looked at the bills again. They weren't brand new, and there was nothing to indicate that they might be counterfeit. And there were ten of them—ten! He fished the envelope out of the trash basket and looked inside. No note, no nothing. He examined the envelope itself: *Herbert Wiggins, Pop's Corner, 116 Washington Street, Baltimore, Maryland.* The return address said merely, *DemocRatic Association of R., PO Box 25aa, Chicago, Illinois.*

Pops picked up the other envelope. This one had a different typeface. The return address was printed in tiny script on the back. Pops fished his reading glasses out of his shirt pocket and perched them on his nose.

His hands shook as he ripped open the letter. There were no bills, he saw at once, and he was almost relieved. He did find a slip of paper, which he pulled out and unfolded. His eyes almost jumped out of their sockets.

Boston R. Society of the ARts
114a Peale Street
Boston, Massachusetts 55543

$1,122.00

Pay to the Order of: ___Herbert Wiggins___

One thousand one hundred and twenty-two dollars and 0 cents

For: club fund Aristotle-R., treasurer

This can't be happening, Pops thought. He remembered the first envelope, which had come last week, and the money he'd stuck in the top right-hand drawer of his desk. He fingered the hundred-dollar bills that lay in his lap and examined the check again. Was someone playing an awful joke on him? Maybe Earlene's idea of asking George the mailman wasn't so bad after all. He gathered the money and envelopes, opened the drawer of his desk, and added them to the two hundred dollars that was already there.

༶

CHAPTER TWENTY-SIX

Twenty-one Days Left, and Counting . . .

WITH SO MANY ROACHES off on missions, others had
to do their work. Demo was asked to look after the oldest roach in the colony, Do-zen. Do-zen had a lifelong
reputation as a rebel. When he was asked which family he
belonged to, he always answered, "I am a citizen of the
world." Now he was almost blind, and hard of hearing.
Sometimes he forgot where he was going, and why. Impy
had once whispered that Do-zen was "doddering."
Demo wasn't sure what that meant. But the good thing
about Do-zen was that he loved to sing. You could keep
track of his wanderings by listening: "*Amazing Grace, how*

sweet the sound, to save a roach like me . . ." would come drifting down the hallway. *"Roach of Ages . . ."* might be heard near the bathroom drainpipe. *"How much is that roachie in the window?"* would squeak from the club pantry. Even so, Demo worried that the old roach might wander off and get lost.

Demo's job began before breakfast. He would help the elder off his sleeping mat and hand him his spectacles.

"Who are you?" Do-zen would ask.

"Demo."

"Lemo?"

"DEMO."

"You needn't shout, my lad."

But a few minutes later, Do-zen would ask: "What's your name?"

"Demo."

"Bemo?"

"DEMO."

"Oh, yes. I remember now."

And a few minutes later, Demo would hear: "What are you called, lad?" and the whole cycle would begin again.

Nevertheless, Demo liked looking after Do-zen. He liked crawling beside him when the old roach scaled the wall, being ready to reach out and grab him if he slipped. He liked finding tiny scraps of food to feed him. The elder would feel the morsel with his feet, because he couldn't see it. Once he said, "Baked potato—that's my favorite. I'd almost forgotten how wonderful it tastes. Thank you, Femo," he added.

Demo just stood there.

Demo followed him from room to room. Do-zen

knew of places Demo had never been. There was a tiny opening in the upstairs ceiling that led to a room he called *the attic*. It was filled with old trunks and cardboard boxes and stacks of magazines. Some contained photographs of faraway countries. Demo turned the pages. Do-zen would peer down through his spectacles, but he really couldn't see. He'd ask Demo to tell him what was there. "Flower," Demo said. "Fountains."

"A tower in the mountains . . . I believe that's Greece," the old roach said. "I traveled there in '89. I went on board a freighter, and the seas were high. I've never been so sick in all my life. At the very first port, I climbed inside a bale of cloth and went ashore. The city was called Athens, and the roaches there were mostly artists and philosophers. . . ."

"Like Socra-Roach?"

"No coaches—they traveled on donkeys. They loved to dance and drink ouzo. Every four years they held athletic games: races and flying matches and kick-the-crumb. . . ."

Do-zen got distracted. He started singing "On Top of Old Roachie." Demo could tell he'd had a fine voice once, and even now he sang on key and with great spirit. When he finished a song, he'd give a little bow, and Demo would clap his two front feet.

Demo loved going to the attic. He saw pictures of places he'd never even heard of, and heard stories to go along with them.

Do-zen had met the roach who had ridden in the Sherpa's pack the day Mount Everest was first climbed; and another who'd hidden himself in the inner folds of the space suit of a Russian cosmonaut and circled the earth for almost a week. He himself had traveled widely. He described the island of Madagascar, where some of Demo's ancestors were from. "Those roaches are the biggest, strongest, and ultimately perhaps the smartest of our breed. They've learned to use their massive size and hisses not to attack but to defend." Do-zen straightened his spectacles and looked Demo up and down. "You are a quiet lad, Wemo," he said. "But in quietness is strength. When you do speak, all will listen to your chosen words."

CHAPTER TWENTY-SEVEN

"Help me!"

SHINY SHOULDN'T HAVE DONE IT. She relived the moment one more time: the pink handbag lying open on the floor by Earlene's bed, where Bitty had dropped it; Bitty and her grandma watching TV; Shiny making a run for it, leaping inside the open purse, hiding herself among the crayons and scraps of paper. Before she'd even had time to reconsider the decision, there was a voice: "Time to go, Bitty." The purse snapped shut. Shiny had swung back and forth, back and forth, as Bitty clomped downstairs. The purse was dark inside; the plastic lining slippery. With each step, Shiny tumbled up and down among bubble gum

99
99

wrappers and broken crayons. A moldy pizza crust smacked against her. "Disgusting," Shiny said out loud. Somewhere in the world, there were roaches so poor that they ate garbage, but she was not among them. She tried to straighten her antennae ribbons so she'd look her best, but it was hopeless. Abruptly the lurching stopped. Something roared, and they all moved forward, this time smoothly. "Were you good at Grandma's?" someone asked.

"No," Bitty answered. "I hate being good. And Troy got more chocolate milk than me. It wasn't fair."

A little later, the motor—Shiny'd figured out they must be in a car—clicked off. Bitty grabbed the purse again. Shiny clung to a crayon. It rolled around the bottom of the pocketbook. A dirty Kleenex covered Shiny like a gooey

blanket. She was so mad she felt like screaming. But who would hear her if she did?

Things got worse. Bitty got into a shouting battle with her mom. Shiny had never heard anybody yell so loud.

"I WON'T!"

"Bitty, if you can't behave, I'll send you to your room."

"I WON'T BEHAVE!"

"Young lady . . ."

Shiny felt the purse—and all its contents—take off like a rocket ship. *BLAM!* They hit something hard. The handbag tumbled, landing on the floor. Shiny was knocked dizzy. "Help!" she called out. "Help!"

"GO TO YOUR ROOM!"

A door slammed. Shiny was crying. "Mama, Papa, Demo, Impy . . ." Bitty was crying too. Her sobs were like earthquakes.

"Help!" Shiny called. "Help me!" But her cries were drowned out by Bitty's own.

CHAPTER TWENTY-EIGHT

Impy Makes Another Mistake

IMPY WAS WORKING HARD in the nursery, taking care of Alicia, Horace, and Peewee. They were growing fast, so they were always hungry and often wet. Every other minute Horace was crying, or Peewee was kicking Alicia, and Alicia was shrieking for him to stop. Sometimes Impy felt like shrieking too. When would these babies learn to behave?

"You were like this too," Bonita explained.

"Not me . . ." Impy was sure he hadn't been. After all, his mom had never said a word about him being fussy or naughty or out of sorts. Nor had she mentioned that about his brothers or sisters. Harlequin nymphs must be especially good.

"I remember you," the nurse continued. "We had to carry you down from the ceiling every other day. You'd get up there and start howling, because you were afraid you'd fall."

"Are you sure that was me?"

Bonita nodded. "We had to keep you in here longer than the rest. And now you're back."

Not 'cause I want to be, Impy felt like saying; but he kept that to himself.

To make things all the more frustrating, last night he'd found a note from Shiny in his bedroll. When he'd gone to look for her this morning, no one could tell him where she was. Her family didn't seem upset. "She's probably some- where learning a new dance," one of her grandmas said.

"But she said she was going on a mission. . . ."

The elder kept right on watching the nymphs in her corner, who were playing kick-the-crumb. "Shiny is a lively nymph, but smart. I'm sure she'll come back safe and sound."

Impy sighed. He wondered where she'd gone. Surely she wasn't dumb enough to get herself lost, or in a dangerous . . . Horace started screaming. Impy picked him up and rocked him. When he put him down, Horace started crying all over again. He shrieked so loud he woke up Peewee and Alicia too. Impy was furious. *"Horace,"* he whispered angrily, *"there is nothing wrong with you! You are just a spoiled brat!"* Horace screamed louder still.

"What's wrong?" Bonita scurried over from the far side of the nursery.

"Impy mean!" Horace yowled. "Calling Horace spoiled brat!"

"Horace, calm down." Bonita picked Horace up and rocked him for a minute. He fell asleep and didn't wake again when she set him in his bed.

It is most unusual for adult roaches to lose their tempers, and Bonita did not. Nevertheless, her shell turned darker, and her antennae flared upright. She took Impy aside. "What did you say to Horace?" she demanded.

Impy knew that he should be ashamed of what he'd done, but instead he was mad. Horace could talk! All along he'd been whining and howling and making Impy guess what was wrong with him, when he could have said *I'm hungry*, or *I want you to pick me up*.

"Horace could have asked for what he needed," he mumbled. Bonita disagreed. "Horace is a baby. It was your job to take care of him, no matter what he did or didn't say."

"Oh." Impy hung his head. But Bonita's words were dancing in his mind: *It was your job* . . . Was he about to be set free?

Bonita continued to scold. Impy picked up bits of what she said: ". . . shall have to report to the Elder Roach Council that this arrangement is unsatisfactory . . . Never before have I seen . . . Not trying to aid a helpless child . . ."

"I wasn't helpless," Impy protested.

"I'm talking about *Horace*."

"Oh." There was a silence during which Impy felt that maybe Bonita hadn't been pleased with his performance.

"You may leave now," she finally said.

"Really?" Impy couldn't believe it. He must have

been wrong about what Bonita thought. "You mean I'm done?"

"We'll see what Socra-Roach says about that."

"Uh-oh."

"Uh-oh is right. Now go to his office and tell him what I said."

The problem was, Impy had been distracted. Now he tried to remember exactly what the nurse had said— he thought *maybe* he remembered: *Never before have I seen . . . such a satisfactory arrangement . . . He was trying to help. . . .* That was it, wasn't it? He felt a little uneasy, so he went over it twice. He wanted to report the words just as Bonita had said them.

The interview with Socra-Roach didn't happen right away. Instead of going straight to Socra-Roach's office, Impy decided he really ought to practice kick-the-crumb. As a result, the Elder had spoken to Bonita before Impy arrived. It turned out her assessment of Impy's work was different from what Impy himself remembered. Some of the words Socra-Roach repeated almost rang a bell, but not quite: un*satisfactory arrangement . . .* Not *trying to aid a helpless child . . .*

"You don't understand," Impy protested. "Horace is whiny. And he pretended he couldn't talk, and then when I called him a spoil—" Impy clamped his mouth shut. Socra-Roach might not like that part of the story. "Uhhhh . . . he said I was mean, after I'd been trying and trying to put him to—"

"I've already heard more than I need to. You're to go back to the nursery and try again."

"That's not fair! Demo has an easier job than I do, and

Shiny's gone—" Impy backpedaled. He hadn't meant to get Shiny into trouble."

What's this about Shiny?"

"Uh . . . nothing."

"Where is Shiny now?"

"I'm not sure . . ."

Socra-Roach was staring right at him.

"I found this note," Impy confessed. "It was tucked inside my sleeping mat." He handed Socra-Roach the tiny paper. The elder studied it carefully. Frown lines creased his already wrinkled face.

"Have you looked for her this morning?"

"Yes, but I couldn't find her."

Socra-Roach looked upset. "Surely she wouldn't have been so foolish as to leave the club."

Impy shuffled from foot to foot. "She was upset because she wasn't on the list. I tried to reason with her, but she told me to shut up."

Socra-Roach banged his walking stick on his desk. Impy had never seen him so mad. The council clerk came running. Socra-Roach's voice was clipped, and he didn't smile or greet the clerk. "All-points bulletin, Shinola Banan, a nymph last seen with ribbons"—he looked over at Impy—"what color ribbons?"

"Silver with sparkles."

". . . last seen with sparkling silver ribbons on her antennae. May have been missing since yesterday. Please alert the community to search the premises and report back immediately."

"Yes, sir." The clerk ran out to spread the word.

"You could have come to me, you know," Socra-Roach said to Impy.

"I didn't know—"

"Even if you *thought* . . ."

Impy hung his head. The day was going from bad to worse. "I can look for her. I know the places she hangs out."

"I'd rather have you in the nursery. That way I'll know exactly where you are, so that you're not in trouble, too."

Impy knew better than to argue. He trudged slowly back to the nursery, where Horace, Alicia, and Peewee were waiting for him.

❦

CHAPTER TWENTY-NINE

Girl Meets Bug

"HELP!" SHINY SCREAMED. She was hysterical. She was trapped in the purse forever. She would probably die here. And no one—not her mother or father, sister or brother, best friend or cousin—would have any idea what had happened to her. They would mourn, of course, but they might think that she'd simply abandoned them for someplace safer and better. "Booo-hooo-hooo," Shiny sobbed, and then she screamed again, as loud as she could: "HELP!"

By then Bitty had quieted. She was lying on her back on the carpet, examining her shoelaces.

"HELP!" Shiny shrieked.

Bitty tied her laces in a knot.

"I'M DYING!" Shiny wailed.

Bitty wiggled all her toes. She was bored. She wondered if there were any good pages left in her coloring book. The problem was, she didn't know where the coloring book was. Maybe she would draw a picture on the wall—just a little one, so she didn't get in too much trouble. She knew where she had crayons . . . She slid her toe under the handle of her pocketbook. She liked picking things up with her toes. She flipped the purse onto her chest and snapped it open.

"Help!"

It was the smallest voice Bitty had ever heard—so small that she wondered if it was really there. Troy was always saying she imagined things. She put her ear to the open pocketbook. Nothing. And yet she was sure . . . almost sure . . . She shook the contents of the purse out on the floor. Pennies, crayons, Kleenex, some bubble gum wrappers . . . They couldn't talk. There was some pizza crust. Bitty sniffed it. Yuck! She threw it under the bed. Nothing else . . . except—

Bitty stared.

The little brown thing had legs. One of them was moving, just slightly. Bitty picked it up and studied it.

"A bug," she whispered.

The bug looked back at her. "HELP!" Its voice was so tiny that Bitty could barely hear it. Then it went limp.

༒

CHAPTER THIRTY

Seventeen Days Left, and Counting . . .

"PATIENCE IS THE HARLEQUIN WAY," Impy's mom said when she heard what happened in the nursery and later in Socra-Roach's office.

"I don't have patience," Impy replied.

"You do—we all do. But sometimes we forget and have to find the way again. Remember how you practiced sounding out the letters until you finally learned to read?"

"But I *wanted* to read. I don't *want* to be a good babysitter. I want to be an explorer."

"You can be an explorer here at home," his mother said.

"How?"

"When I was a nymph, my friends and I pretended we were cowboys or explorers or astronauts. I still remember how much fun we had."

"Those were just games!"

"Playing prepares you for what you might do later. And besides, adults play too."

"They do?"

"Of course. They make up stories and dance and play kick-the-crumb, just like nymphs."

"I never thought of that."

His mother smiled. "Patience," she repeated.

Impy took his time thinking about what he wanted to do as a grown-up roach and how he could practice those skills now. He imagined himself as a movie star, a Shakespearean actor, the drummer in a rock-and-roll band. But one career appealed to him above all else: secret agent.

It was a job he could start now. Some older roaches, like his mom, might assume that it was all a game; but he had no intention of playing. Instead he would train himself to be a real spy. He got to work, signing his name over and over until it felt natural: *Impetuous Roach, FBI*. He figured out his alias: Impy, a short, smart nymph who worked in the nursery. Only he would know his true identity—and he would never reveal it. So the more that others thought he was just a runty nymph, the better.

He no longer dreaded being in the nursery, because it was important to maintain his alias. Peewee and Alicia, who didn't know that anything had changed, were glad to see him. Their faces lit up, and they started waving their tiny antennae. "Impy's here! Impy's here!" Sure, the stories he made up for them were dumb, but even so, Impy had to feel a little bit pleased by the delight the nymphs—including Horace—seemed to take in them, and the way they shouted, "Tell 'nother, tell 'nother," as soon as a story was done. Time in the nursery passed more quickly. Bonita was happier with Impy's work. And when his hours were over, he went off to skulk about the building.

He spied on everyone. Of course, most of the routines were familiar: the games of kick-the-crumb, the afternoon naps, the meetings of the Elder Roach Council. Pops's work, too, was fairly predictable: sweeping the club floor, wiping down the counters, checking the sound system, calling the city paper to tell them who was playing at the club, and when. For an hour or so Pops sat in his office. He smoked a cigar, read his mail, ordered beer for the performances, and called up bands to make sure the plans he'd made with them were understood. Impy tagged along behind him. That was how he happened to overhear Pops's conversation with the mailman, George.

"What is it, Pops?" The mailman was impatient. His stomach sagged below his belt, and he wore black plastic glasses with big frames.

"I've been getting letters that aren't for me." Pops held out some envelopes, and George examined them.

"They've got your name and address on them."

"But it's a mistake. Whoever's sending them thinks I'm someone else."

"How do you know?"

"Because I've never met these people—not one of them—and they're sending me something valuable. And there's no explanation, no letter or note or anything." Pops didn't intend to tell George the whole truth, not with George's big mouth. "I'm wondering if the post office can trace the addresses and see whether they're real. That way I can write and tell them I'm not who they think I am."

"Why don't you just keep it, whatever it is?"

"Because it isn't mine."

George snorted. The sound reminded Impy of a donkey's hee-haw. "This doesn't make sense. I'm telling you, man, these have your name on them, and your address."

"No one sends money to a stranger."

"Money?"

Pops cringed. He hadn't meant to let the word slip out. But George went on: "You should keep it, Pops. We all know the club's in trouble."

"Why do you say that?"

"There was a fellow snooping around last week. Told Mrs. Murry he's going to buy the building from the bank in a few weeks when they foreclose."

Pops was silent.

"Look, maybe you've got a secret admirer. Think of the things you've done for people in the neighborhood—all the times you put an empty jar at the register because someone was laid off, or out of heating oil, or in the hospital."

"Sometimes I did, but other times it was Earlene. Anyway, these letters are from far away. If I keep the money, next thing you know, the police will arrest me for stealing."

"Then tell the police! I'm just a mailman delivering what's addressed to you."

"Maybe I will," Pops sighed. The last thing he wanted was the police coming around, checking on his licenses and permits. He closed the door in disgust and strode back toward his office.

Impy followed him. Where did Pops keep the envelopes? Who were they from? And how much money did they contain?

CHAPTER THIRTY-ONE

⟨❧⟩

"Alive!"

SHINY HAD FAINTED, so she didn't hear Bitty sobbing.
Her cries were so noisy that they echoed through the house.
Finally Troy banged on the bedroom door.

"Bitty, shut up! I can't hear my music."

"I won't shut up!"

"What's wrong?"

"I killed it." Bitty's small shoulders shook.

Troy opened the door a little bit. "Killed what?"

"Look . . ."

Troy came closer. He peered at the small object in
Bitty's hand. "That's gross! Throw it in the trash!"

"I won't!"

"If Mom sees a roach in here—"

"It's dead!"

"Crying over a dead bug! You're crazy!" Troy left, slamming the door behind him. The noise roused Shiny. She lifted her head and looked around, unable to remember where she was. A high squeal split the air. Shiny looked up and saw Bitty's face above her.

"You're not dead!" Bitty shouted.

Shiny didn't answer.

"You're alive! And you can talk!"

Shiny stayed still. She wasn't sure what to do.

"You can be my pet. I wanted a kitty. Daddy said no, but I won't tell him about—"

"Bitty . . ." The voice that drifted from the other room was gentle. Even so, Bitty recoiled slightly. What was it Troy had said? *If Mom sees a roach in here . . .* She picked Shiny up quickly and stuck her in her dollhouse.

"Bitty . . ."

"What, Mom?"

"Time for supper."

"I'll be right there."

The door closed, and Shiny was alone.

Shiny looked around in wonder. The only place she'd ever lived was Pops's, so she'd assumed that everywhere else was just like it. But she'd been wrong. Here was a house designed for her. It had a little bed, a chair, a table. There were drapes on the windows and a door that opened and closed. There was a kitchen like Pops and Earlene's, only

this kitchen was roach-size. There was even a little cup-
board with tiny plates and cups. Shiny ran up and down the
steps, from the first floor to the second, the second to the
third, and back again. There were three bedrooms, ample
space for five or six roach families. Nymphs could sleep in
the little bathtubs. There was a pool table, a television, and
a stereo. Shiny tried to turn it on. It didn't start. Bitty must
have forgotten to pay the electric bill. Pops had done the
same thing this spring. For almost two days the club had
been dark. She and the other nymphs had had a wonderful

time playing hide-and-seek and telling scary stories. They'd pretended to be Creepies and jumped out at each other, yelling, "Stick 'em up!" Finally Pops had gone downtown with a pocketful of money. That very day the lights were turned back on.

She would talk to Bitty, Shiny decided. But for now she lay back in the little wooden bed. She pulled the coverlet up over her, rested her head on the tiny pillow, and fell asleep.

CHAPTER THIRTY-TWO

The Investigation

SECRET AGENT IMPETUOUS R. could hardly wait until nightfall, when he could search for the mysterious letters. But Pops and Earlene didn't go to bed till ten, even when the club was closed. Impy kept waiting to hear Pops's shoes go upstairs to the apartment. The clock said ten minutes after ten. Impy tried breathing deeply and repeating, "Patience, patience, patience." When he opened his eyes, the clock said twelve minutes after ten. He couldn't wait a second longer. He ran underneath the office door and scurried up the wall, taking shelter behind a photograph of John Coltrane.

The lights were off, but the end of Pops's cigar glowed

orange in the ashtray on the desk. Pops was sitting in his chair. The radio played a Billie Holiday song. Her voice rose and fell in the darkness. There was a feeling of sadness under the words she sang. An old black-and-white photograph of her hung behind the bar, between Louis Armstrong and Charlie Parker. "*So many heartaches*," she sang now. "*So many heartaches.*"

After a bit Pops turned off the stereo. He sighed, stubbed out the cigar, and left. Impy heard his feet plod slowly up the stairs.

Impy got to work. He checked the trash can for the envelopes Pops had described. He looked on the desktop, but most of what he found were bills. There was a new threat from the bank. Printed in black letters, it read:

AUCTION DATE FOR 116 WASHINGTON STREET HAS BEEN SET FOR TUESDAY THE 11TH OF AUGUST AT TWELVE NOON. SIGNS WILL BE POSTED ON THE PREMISES TWO WEEKS BEFORE THE EVENT. BUILDING WILL BE OPEN FOR INSPECTION FROM 9:00 A.M. ON THE DAY OF SALE.

August 11? That was only sixteen days away! Impy's heart thumped. And he knew that if he was scared, it must be ten times worse for Pops.

He kept searching. Finally, in the top right desk drawer, he found four letters. The most recent was postmarked three days ago and came from BSR of America, 32 Holden Way, Cleveland, Ohio. It was addressed to Herbert Wiggins. And inside, neatly folded, were seven one-hundred-dollar bills.

The other three letters were clipped together just beneath it. The writing in the left-hand corner was different on each one. Impy looked inside the envelopes. The letter from Chicago contained another thousand dollars in cash; the Boston one a check for $1,122; and the envelope from Philadelphia held two hundred dollars in twenty-dollar bills. If Impy's figuring was correct, as of tonight Pops's desk drawer contained roughly three thousand dollars!

But who had sent the money? BSR of AmeRica, BPOR, Boston R. Society of the ARts, DemocRatic Association of R . . . They had something in common, Impy was sure of it. He lay back on his shell so he could think. He'd heard of the Boy Scouts of America, but not the BSR of America. There was something just a little bit wrong with all these names, and it had to do with the letter R.

It wasn't until he looked at the money one last time that he caught on. The signature on the check read ARistotle-R. The name was Greek, Impy was pretty sure. He and the others had donated a quarter of the sum Pops needed to pay off his debts. Yet Pops didn't think the money was his and wasn't going to use it. Impy's mind raced. Was it possible this money *had* been sent to stop the auction? He must tell Socra-Roach immediately, he decided. *Socra-Roach . . . Aristotle-R . . . Socra-Roach . . . Aristotle-R . . . Socra-Roach . . . Aristotle-Roa . . .*

"Oh, my goodness!" Impy said out loud.

∽∾

CHAPTER THIRTY-THREE

The Benefit

THE PHONE RANG INSISTENTLY, but Pops didn't feel like answering it. That same morning a man from the auction house had posted a notice for auction sign on the building. Pops had taken it down, but not before it had been seen. What he had wanted most was to spare Earlene the news about the club and the fact that she and Pops might have to move. Now that seemed impossible.

The phone kept ringing. Pops threw down his broom in disgust, went into his office, and picked it up. The voice on the other end was vaguely familiar.

"This is Newt Carson, from the KitKats."

Pops had to push himself to mumble, "How you doin', Newt?"

"Better than you, man. Word is the club is going down. The boys and me decided we're not going to let that happen."

On the other end of the phone Pops was silent.

"We talked to a bunch of bands. We want to play a concert at the club two weeks from now. We'll charge a lot for the tickets, and all the proceeds will go to you."

Pops was silent.

"No one has to know that you need cash. We'll call it a benefit to promote historic landmarks. After all, Pop's Corner is the oldest jazz club in the city."

"Ummm . . ." Pops felt touched. He'd felt so alone, but now he saw that there were people who cared, people whom he hardly even knew. Still, there was no way he was taking someone's else's charity.

"You helped us, man. Give us a chance to help *you* out."

The young man was so eager that Pops almost said yes. But in the long run, he couldn't. The club was his responsibility. If it failed, that was his fault and no one else's.

CHAPTER THIRTY-FOUR

❧

The True Histories of Michelangelo, Leonardo da Vinci, and Beethoven

IMPY WAS SITTING IN FRONT of Socra-Roach's office door when the Elder arrived. Impy shouted—as if Socra-Roach were deaf—"I FOUND THREE THOUSAND DOLLARS!"

"WHAT? Where?"

"IN POPS'S DRAWER!"

"Hold on, there. And stop shouting! What were you doing in Pops's desk?"

"I was investigating . . . You see, I heard Pops tell the mailman he'd been—"

"That's his private space," Socra-Roach said.

"But he's got this money, and I think . . ." Impy told Socra-Roach exactly what he'd overheard, and about his decision to investigate. He described the envelopes. "They came from Philadelphia, Chicago, Boston, and Cleveland. And there were initials in the corner—"

"You mean the return address."

Impy nodded. "Some are from groups I've heard of, only the initials aren't quite right. Instead of Boy Scouts of America, one of them was BSR of America, and another was an art society, only it was Boston R. Society of the Arts. They sent a check from Aristotle-R."

Impy drew the figure R as it appeared on the envelopes.

"That looks like a form of roach script. Who did you say signed the check?"

"Aristotle-R."

"Did the letter come from Peale Street?"

Impy stopped to think. "Yes, I'm pretty sure it did."

The old roach grabbed his walking stick. "I want to see this for myself."

Pops was mopping the bathroom floor. "About time," Socra-Roach sniffed as they scurried by. "It was filthy in there." He and Impy scooted under the office door and up onto the desk. Impy showed Socra-Roach the letter about the auction. Then he pointed out the drawer with the money inside it. Socra-Roach nodded.

"You stay out here," he said. "If Pops comes in and closes the drawer, you'll know where I am and can get help."

When Socra-Roach came back out, Impy could see that something had changed. The elder's antennae, which usually drooped with age, were upright, and his walking stick tapped fast. He signaled for Impy to follow him into a crack behind the paneling.

"Impetuous Roach," he said, "you have made a very important discovery."

Socra-Roach was pretty sure where the money had come from. "In the United States and elsewhere, roach communities are united by family ties, like ours. But there are other groups who join together, too. The Boston Roach Society of the Arts is a group of painters and sculptors who became interested in the art of Michelroachio, who lived in Italy in the fourteen and fifteen hundreds. I needn't tell you that he had his human imitators. So did another genius, Leonardo da Roachi. The museum on Peale Street in Boston contains some of their great works and is governed by a board of elders that includes Aristotle, my fourteenth cousin on my Uncle Plato's side."

"But where did they get human money?"

"Some groups accumulated large sums by selling works of art, literature, and music that could be adapted by human beings. Beethoven's ninth symphony, for example, was really the work of a tiny collective of roach composers who lived in Berlin in the seventeen hundreds. They slipped the score to a young human musician, who made it his own, so to speak. But he was well aware of his debt to the roaches, and he shoved a tidy sum into the crevice in his bedroom floor. Invested over the long term, the proceeds have been substantial."

Impy was confused. "Is the money kept in banks?"

"No, they use stock markets. Brokers have always been willing to take money without seeing the owners—it can be mailed or wired with instructions for investments. People refuse to acknowledge this, but the crash of 1929 here in the U.S. was really caused by the invention of a particularly cruel insecticide. Roaches got fed up and pulled their money from the markets. Unfortunately, some innocent humans suffered for the meanness of those scientists and the exterminating companies to whom they sold their product."

"I never knew that."

"Few roaches do. We don't want to flaunt our power, so we keep it quiet."

"But . . . what about the BSR of America? I thought those letters stood for Boy Scouts."

"There are roach scouts, too. They dress in brown and camp out in the woods, where they eat chocolate. The female members sell sweet snacks. That's how they make their money."

"What about the BPOR?"

"The Benevolent and Protective Order of Roaches is a social club. They have monthly meetings where they share food and fellowship."

"Why would *they* send money to Pops?"

"Because of our collective intelligence. Remember our rule about helping roaches in need? We believe when one roach is in trouble, all the rest of us are too; so we help each other. That's why our species has survived so long. In this case, the BPOR must have heard about our situation."

"How did they hear? Did we ask for help?"

Socra-Roach looked puzzled. "Not really. We tried setting up a Web site, but we didn't have the credit card information that was needed, so we couldn't do it." The old roach sat thinking. Finally he shook his head. "I can't imagine how the others learned about our problems. If you hadn't overheard the conversation with the mailman and looked inside the desk, we wouldn't have known about the money."

"Pops thinks it's a mistake."

"We'll have to let him know it's not. I'll talk that over with the council. In the meantime, we'll need to make sure Pops doesn't give the money to the police, or mail it back."

CHAPTER THIRTY-FIVE

Creepies

DO-ZEN WANTED to go outside.

"Nope," Demo said. Dusk was falling; it would soon be dark.

"Temo, you needn't shout so loud. I *want* you to come with me. The maple tree is lovely in the night." By now Do-zen was partway down the outside screen. For a moment Demo just stood there. Then he realized he had to follow the elder, even though it was against the rules. What if Do-zen got lost or hurt?

But the old roach climbed deftly to the ground. He positioned himself under the boughs of the tree. Demo stood beside him, looking up. The branches shone shiny black through the light of the rising moon. Do-zen started singing an old song, "Beautiful Dreamer." His voice was lovely. Demo felt as if he were in a trance. Then—suddenly— he heard a rustle to his right. Shadows moved swiftly.

"Stick 'em up," somebody yelled.

The shadows were roaches, Demo saw now: Creepies. They wore their hats pulled low over their faces. One of them grabbed Do-zen's spectacles and put them on himself.

"Look at me! I'm an old fart!"

The others laughed.

Demo just stood there.

"Give those back," Do-zen yelped.

"What was that, Grandpa?"

"Back off, boys—" A female voice penetrated the darkness. "Thuggy, give the old roach his glasses back."

"How come?"

"'Cause he's a geezer." The gang's leader stepped closer. Her shell shone bright green in the moonlight.

Do-zen put his spectacles back on and then adjusted them. He moved closer to the Creepies' boss. "What's your name?" he asked.

"Czarina Pepina. And yours, Grandpa?"

"Do-zen, at your service." The elder gave a little bow.

"Cool. I wish I had more time to chat, but this *is* a robbery, you know."

"They ain't got nuthin'," the smallest Creepie said.

"Maybe the birdbrain does."

"Shut up, Axel. Don't you see how big he is?"

"I ain't scairt of nobody."

"Then how come you're a-shakin'?"

"Quiet, boys." Czarina Pepina turned to Demo and Do-zen. "You're on Creepie turf," she said sternly. "There's a bounty on our property. We won't let you go till you pay up."

"They ain't got nuthin', boss," the roach called Shorty said.

"Everyone has something." She turned to the captives. "What'll it be?" she asked.

Demo was terrified, but Do-zen didn't seem to understand. "Such beauty demands a song," he said gallantly. " I shall sing "O Roachie Mio." He launched into the melody. All the smaller Creepies turned and stared. Some of them pulled their hats down over their ears. "How do you stand this old-time stuff?" Shorty whispered to Demo. "Can't you teach him some hip-hop?"

"The boss is having fun," Thuggy murmured.

Sure enough, Czarina was twirling and spinning to the music. But when Do-zen reached the end of the last chorus, she lay down on the ground.

"I'm whipped," she said.

"We ain't going to jack nobody up?"

"No, we've had enough excitement for one night." She glanced at Demo. "Where you dudes from, anyway?"

Demo pointed to the club. Its pink neon sign outlined the words *Pop's Corner*, then flowed into the bell end of a saxophone. "You're part of the Socratic gang," Czarina said.

"Nope," Demo said.

Do-zen seemed to understand. "We aren't a gang," he started to explain. "We're families who live together in the same—"

"*Bor—ing!*" The other Creepies shook their heads. "Don't you ever fight, or rob? What do you do for fun?"

"K—k—kick-the-crumb," Demo stuttered.

"Kick-the-crumb!" The Creepies nearly fell down laughing. "That's so old-time!"

Czarina Pepina made them stop. She turned to Demo

and Do-zen. "Go home," she said. "And tell old Socra this: a plan's afoot to rip Pops off."

Demo knew she must be wrong, 'cause Pops was broke. But she went on: "If you come back on Creepie turf, we'll have to dust you up."

"Can't we beat them up right now?" Shorty asked.

"Not this time."

"But we ain't scairt of 'em, are we?"

"'Course not. We ain't scairt of nuthin'."

The Creepies strutted away.

CHAPTER THIRTY-SIX

❧

The Perfect Home

SHINY WAS HAPPY in the dollhouse. The first night Bitty brought her corn bread crumbs for supper and a bottle cap of water. Bitty played music on her radio. Shiny didn't know all the songs, of course, but she knew some of them. She danced, wiggling her antennae so that her ribbons made circles in the air around her. Although she felt guilty about her friends and family back home, she had to admit that she'd never had so much fun.

The next morning began on a good note. Shiny slept well. When she awoke, she saw a handful of granola piled neatly on the dining room table. Shiny sat in a chair and ate the cereal with her two front legs, like a human would. She wished she had a little napkin to wipe her mouth, but the ones on the table were just painted there. Oh, well . . . perhaps she could ask Bitty to cut some real ones from a bit of cloth.

Bitty was feeling expansive. She wanted to teach Shiny everything she knew. "There are seven days in the week," she said, and listed them. Shiny had been taught that too, but it was fun to listen to Bitty anyway. The girl went on: "This is Saturday, when we stay home with Mom and Dad. Sometimes the four of us sing together. My mom used to sing at Grandpa's club. That's where Daddy met her."

Shiny asked, "Which song is your favorite?"

Bitty didn't hear, because Shiny's voice was only audible when she bellowed at the top of her lungs. Bitty went on with her lesson. "On Saturday we shop for groceries. I like to go because I get some candy. After I eat the candy, then I can be bad."

"Why are you bad?" Shiny asked.

"The other thing we do on Saturday is clean the house. We're all supposed to help. But sometimes I pretend I'm sick, so I don't have to."

Shiny just listened.

"I don't like work. Troy doesn't mind it. He puts the dishes in the dishwasher and takes the trash out too."

Bitty looked thoughtful now. "Troy's good. I think that's stupid."

"Bitty . . ." The voice was Bitty's mother calling from someplace in the house.

"I'm not answering," Bitty whispered.

She ran out to play in the backyard.

Next time the bedroom door opened, Shiny was expecting Bitty. Instead Bitty's mother came in pushing an odd-looking device. It had a long cord, which she stuck into the wall. The machine itself consisted of a broad metal base, which seemed to roll, with a sort of cloth bag above it, and some switches on the handle. When it was turned on, the machine roared. Shiny noticed old Cheerios and bits of paper flying into it. She'd seen Pops with something similar—Earlene called it a vacuum cleaner. But the one Pops had didn't work half as well as this one, so he mostly used a broom and dustpan, which even the slowest roaches could outrun. Shiny sat on the sofa inside the dollhouse and watched Bitty's mother work.

She began by cleaning the floor under the bed. The machine sucked out crayons and pizza crusts and puzzle pieces. It sucked out a pair of socks, which were grabbed before they went inside the bag. It swallowed a shoestring and several pennies. Bitty's mom looked into the wastebasket, which was empty. She fluffed up the pillow and made the bed. Shiny wondered if she should make *her* bed. She watched from her perch on the sofa as books were put away and dirty clothes tossed in a hamper.

But Bitty's mother wasn't done. She attached a hose to the machine and put a V-shaped piece of plastic on top of it. She ran this along the blinds, sucking up dust, and then along the baseboards of the room. Shiny watched as the woman's feet, clad in blue tennis shoes, stopped next to the dollhouse. On the floor was a trail of granola. The vacuum

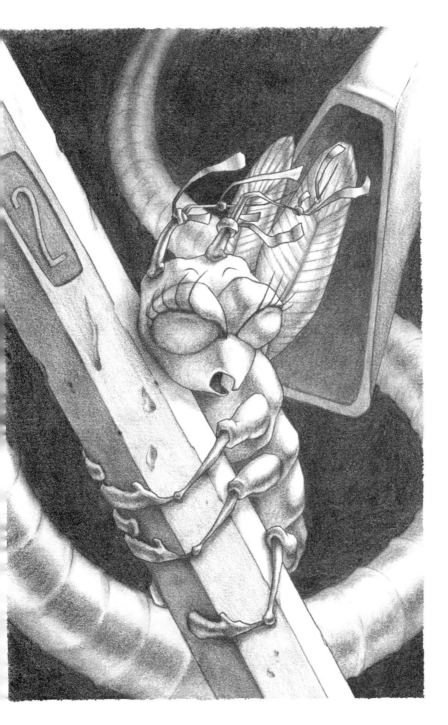

ate it. Suddenly Shiny felt the dollhouse rise. It tipped precariously. The rest of the granola fell out. Shiny clung to the couch, but it started sliding. Then it clattered to the bedroom floor.

For a moment Shiny was stunned. She heard a scream: "Roaches!"

Shiny fled, but the vacuum came right behind her.

She had heard of hurricanes and tornadoes, but she didn't think that they could be as bad as this. Her wings were nothing against the gale-force wind, and her six feet were swept along like tiny grains of sand. She could see the dark mouth of the vacuum coming closer. She screamed, but of course no one could hear. Not that Bitty's mother would be merciful. In fact she seemed to be aiming the hose directly at Shiny.

For the second time in two days, she was sure her life was lost. Tumbling head over tail into the black maw of the vacuum, she grabbed at something flying by. That something was a yellow pencil. Shiny held on to it with all six legs. She said a prayer and closed her eyes.

CHAPTER THIRTY-SEVEN

❧

Troy's Confession

THE PHONE RANG when Troy and his father, Charlie, were playing checkers on the patio. Troy was pretty sure he was about to win. "Let's don't answer," he suggested. But his dad was waiting for a business call. He went inside, got the phone, and brought it outside to the table. Troy could hear the conversation on both ends.

"You don't know me, man, but I'm in a band, and your pops once helped us out. . . ."

"Yes?" Troy's dad was waiting for the other call.

"Last week we heard the club is going down."

Charlie's face was a question mark. "I don't know what you're talking about."

"It's true, man. We called Pops and asked if we could do a benefit to help him out, but he said no. That's why I'm calling you."

"I think there must be some mistake. My father would have told me if there were a problem."

"Check it out, man, and give us a call if we can help. Pops doesn't even need to know."

"I will." Charlie wrote down the young man's name and number. He hung up the phone, stunned.

"It's true, Dad," Troy said. "Every single thing he says is true."

And Troy told his father what he knew.

Troy's parents were horrified. Charlie blamed himself for being so involved with his own work that he hadn't even noticed the club's problems. "It's my fault," he said. "But you could have told us, Troy. That place means everything to Mom and Dad."

"I . . . I didn't know what to do. I was sure Grandpa wanted it to be a secret." Troy swallowed.

"You're probably right. The old codger's stubborn as a goat. He wouldn't admit he needed something if it killed him." Troy's father shook his head. "I'll call Mom. She may know what's going on."

"She doesn't—at least, I don't think so. She's always giving me money to buy soda and potato chips."

"I grew up in that club. It's where I met Zeena, where we got married, where—"

"Calm down, Charlie." Troy's mom took his father's hand. "Now we know, and we can help."

"There's someone else who's trying to help, too." Troy said. "I found a letter on the closet floor."

"Who was it from?"

"The Louis Armstrong Institute. Want to see it?"

"I certainly do."

Charlie was as puzzled by the letter as Troy had been. He read it out loud, as if that would help explain the meaning. "If he wouldn't tell us, who would Pops have told about the debt?" they asked each other. "And why in the world wouldn't that person have known that Louis Armstrong was dead?"

Troy shrugged. "I couldn't figure that out either. I showed the letter to Mr. Foley at the bank—"

"Mr. Foley?"

"Oh." Troy took a deep breath. "I visited the bank," he said softly. And he told his parents what had happened there.

They weren't really mad at Troy—they understood that he hadn't wanted to give away Grandpa's secret. On the other hand, they were astounded that he'd known and done things they had no idea about. The morning he'd claimed to be sick and then gone to the bank instead was a sore point, and they agreed that Troy would be punished for lying. He couldn't tell them that he didn't mind being punished, because he was so relieved that they knew everything, and that the burden of the secret—and what to do about it—was now shared.

CHAPTER THIRTY-EIGHT

❧

Two Weeks Left, and Counting . . .

DEMO DIDN'T TELL ANYONE about meeting the Creepies, because he didn't want to get in trouble. He shouldn't have let Do-zen go outside, but controlling the elder's wanderings was near impossible. Now Do-zen wanted to climb out the window again, to see the beautiful Czarina Pepina. He wanted to take the bus downtown to the museum of art. He wanted to visit the baseball game and search the stands for cast-off fries when it was over. All these ideas were dangerous. So when he also said that he wanted to go upstairs to the apartment, Demo agreed.

He followed Do-zen up the wallpaper, ready to catch the

elder if he should slip. He followed him through the dust balls under the bureau. He lay down beside him while they watched TV. They laughed along with Earlene during reruns of *I Love Lucy*. They watched a French chef make omelets and an apple tart. They were just about to see a Western when the phone rang. Earlene clicked the TV off. "Hello, Charlie," she said. Demo listened in.

"A surprise party for Pops? What a wonderful idea! I won't say a word. I'm excited already. I haven't been to a good party in a long, long time."

After he'd led Do-zen back to his sleeping mat to take a nap, Demo looked for Impy. On his way, he thought about Earlene's conversation. How strange that Charlie was planning to have the party only two days before the auction . . . Demo stopped short. A group of explorers had returned the night before and stood talking on the drainpipe. Rumors of their findings had already circulated: South Street, Philadelphia, was overrun with other insects; the casinos in Atlantic City were cleaned constantly with heavy-duty vacuums; some of the small towns had grown so empty that all the restaurants were out of business. There were a few possibilities: the basement of a Wal-Mart outside Wilmington, and a reducing spa that refused to use chemical pesticides, and served only food that was healthy and organic. "It's mostly lettuce, with a few tomatoes and a bit of cheese," Meg Maddie, explained to Felix. "We might starve to death if we went there."

Then the adults noticed Demo listening, and they quickly changed the subject.

CHAPTER THIRTY-NINE

Home at Last

SHINY COWERED IN THE POCKETBOOK. The pencil
that had saved her life by lodging crosswise in the vacuum's
mouth lay near her on the floor, under the bed. Bitty had
kicked it there. She'd thrown the biggest tantrum ever,
because her mother was a murderer.

Zeena wouldn't listen. "Roaches are dirty," she'd told
Bitty. "I won't have them in this house."

"You're a killer," Bitty said.

"Stay in your room until I tell you to come out."

Bitty ran inside and slammed the bedroom door.

Bitty had no idea that Shiny had survived. Shiny had to

figure out a way to tell her. She thought and thought. Finally she used a scrap of paper from the pocketbook to write a note. Bitty's pink nail polish lay open on the bureau. Shiny used it as ink, dipping her foreleg into the bottle. That night she put the note on Bitty's pillow. In the morning Bitty found it. She spelled out the letters and asked Troy what they meant. "Take me home." Troy was in a hurry; he had a soccer game in fifteen minutes, and he couldn't find his cleats.

Bitty sat down on her chair. She thought about what Troy had said. Then she spoke out loud, softly, as if she were reasoning with herself. "It wasn't on my pillow when I went to bed. . . ."

She sat a minute more.

"Who could have put it there?" she asked. She spent a long time thinking about that.

"Mom didn't put it there," she said. "Or Dad, or Troy, because they *are* at home. I didn't put it there, 'cause I can only write my name."

After a while she said, "The writing is very small—the smallest I've ever seen."

And then: "Maybe *she* wrote this note, asking me to take her home."

Shiny wanted to run out of the purse and nod her head, but of course she didn't dare.

"Dead roaches can't write."

Bitty started giggling. She put both hands over her mouth so no one would hear. "I think you're alive," she whispered. "If you are—and if you're listening—I *will* take you home. I'm going back to Grandma's tomorrow, and I'll bring my pocketbook along."

*　*　*

Bitty was true to her word. The next morning she went to Earlene's, carrying her purse. She and Troy and Grandma watched cartoons. Halfway through the program Bitty announced, "I have to go to the bathroom." She took her handbag with her. After she'd closed the bathroom door, she opened the pocketbook, held out her hand, and waited.

Shiny felt the familiar air of home flood into her veins. No place—nothing—had ever smelled that good. Ignoring Bitty's outstretched hand, she jumped onto the sink and ran down the outside of the drainpipe. It took Bitty a minute to realize what had happened.

"Wait a minute! I want to say good-bye!"

Shiny didn't want to wait an instant more. She turned quickly and waved her foreleg. Then she dashed through a hole in the bathroom paneling. Behind her, Bitty began to cry. After a while Troy heard and came to the bathroom door.

"What's wrong?"

"My bug . . . she ran away."

He came inside. Bitty was on her knees, staring into the tiny hole.

"Your bug is dead. Anyway, roaches are gross."

"She was special, Troy. For one thing, she could talk."

"Bitty . . ."

"That's how I found her. And she could write too. Look—" Bitty showed Troy the tiny note. He examined it.

"Bitty, I don't know where you got this. The name— *Shinola*—sounds like floor polish. And *Miss Adventure*?"

"My bug wrote that! She was hiding in my pocketbook

because Mom tried to kill her! And she wanted me to bring her here."

Troy sighed deeply. "You're in dreamland, Bitty."

But he couldn't stop staring at the tiny note.

CHAPTER FORTY

She's Back!

"GO AWAY," IMPY MUMBLED FROM his sleeping mat. Someone was poking him. He'd been up all night spying, so he was tired.

"Shut up, Imp," somebody said.

"Go awa—" He leaped up from his bed. "Shiny!"

She twirled around and did a few flamenco steps. "I'm back!"

Impy ran and found Demo. Do-zen was napping, so the three of them sat down nearby. Shiny told the others her adventures: about her plan to go to Bitty's house, the time inside the pocketbook, Bitty's kindness, the wonderful roach house, her escape from the vacuum cleaner, and the note she'd left on Bitty's pillow.

"You left a note? What if she shows it to someone?"

Shiny hadn't thought of that. But it didn't matter: "Her family thinks I'm dead." She twirled around again: How good it felt to be home!

"I'll never leave here again," she promised.

"Don't be so sure . . . We're still looking for a place to move."

And Impy filled her in on everything.

CHAPTER FORTY-ONE

The Secret

BEHIND THE SCENES—and mostly out of the roaches' earshot—phone calls crisscrossed each other like an elaborate spiderweb. There were calls between the bank and the auction house, between bands and jazz fans and radio stations, between Troy's house and carpenters and security guards and soundmen. E-mails were sent to musicians in Philadelphia and New York City, and to the Baltimore Historical Society. At the bank, Mr. Foley paid to have three hundred tickets printed. When Earlene heard the admission price, she almost dropped the phone.

"A hundred dollars each! Charlie, what in the world are you thinking?"

"That's not so high these days."

"Not for a fancy place, I guess, but no one will pay that to come here. Have you looked in the lounge lately? That stage is as swaybacked as the old gray mare. The paint is chipping everywhere. And Herbert spends money on the sound system every week, just patching it together so it will run."

"Don't worry, Mom."

Earlene was silent for a moment.

"Charlie, is Herbert behind on the bills? Is that why we're having the party? Tell me the truth, please."

"He's a couple months behind . . ."

"*That's* why he's been so quiet."

"Mom, I don't want you to worry. We'll make the money back, and more."

Earlene sighed. This wasn't the first time the club had been in debt. She got right down to business: "How much time do we have until the money's due?"

"Nine days."

"That's enough. We won't have to pay for food. The neighbors are making deviled eggs and biscuits and fried chicken."

"How did they find out?"

"I mentioned the party to Betty Jones. I'm afraid she has a big mouth. In the last few days, I've had twenty people call."

"Let them know they're all invited as our guests. Maybe they can help you get Dad out of the club that day. When you come back at night, we'll be ready for you."

"I'll figure something out."

But Earlene knew it would be hard. Pops wouldn't want to spend a single cent on going out. And she'd have to come up with a plan that wasn't too exhausting. She didn't want to miss a second of the party.

"Earlene," Pops said that evening during supper. "Somebody moved my radio."

"I didn't." Earlene tried to look innocent. She studied the butter on her bread.

"It's sat on the same shelf for thirty years!"

"Oh, I remember now—Charlie decided to get it fixed because the sound is fuzzy."

"That radio is fine! I'm missing my programs—'Jazz Beat' and 'In the Swing.' I listen to them every week, to keep up with the music news."

"It won't hurt you to miss them once or twice. And when Charlie brings it back, the radio will sound like it's brand new."

"It sounded good!" Pops fumed. "If I'd needed it replaced, I would have done it on my own."

Earlene waited till the meal was done to bring up her idea. Pops had pulled his easy chair beside the bed and flicked on the TV.

They'd watched a couple minutes of the news. Then Earlene had taken the remote and turned the TV off.

Pops was surprised. "I thought you liked that show. That's why I put it on."

"I do like it. But there's something I want to talk to you about."

She smiled at Pops. He looked uncomfortable.

"I'd like to go to church a week from now, on August ninth. They're having a special service that morning, starting at eight o'clock. And I need you to take me there."

"To church?" Pops said his prayers, of course, but he usually stayed home on weekend mornings.

Earlene went on: "Afterward I'm hoping we can eat breakfast at the pancake house. You know my church friends all go there. You can get the hearty-man platter, the one with the bacon and sausages."

"Uhhh . . ." Pops didn't want to tell Earlene they didn't have the money.

"And Zeena got free passes to the movies. There's one I'd like to see at two, and another at four thirty."

"But we'd be gone all day," Pops grumped. "I'm afraid that it will be too much for you."

"I'll take some extra pills. And it will be a day that's just for us. Think about it, Herbert: how long has it been since we've had one of those?"

Pops did think about it. He'd go, he decided, and hope she would have fun. Because when they came home that night, he'd have to tell her the awful awful truth: the club was closing. They'd have to move. He swallowed. He didn't know if he could say the words to her.

"What do you think?"

"Uh . . . sure, I guess." His voice was hoarse. "I think I'd better go downstairs and sweep the floor."

He waited until he was inside his office to let the tears swell up, and then he brushed them angrily away.

❦

CHAPTER FORTY-TWO

Six Days Left, and Counting . . .

EVERYONE WAS PLEASED THAT Shiny had come home. There were some who felt she should be reprimanded for her foolishness and for the worry she had caused. Socra-Roach agreed. She would replace Impy in the nursery, he decided. Shiny pretended to pout, but she was so glad to be home that she didn't really mind. To add to her happiness, Carlita had embraced her, pressing her bright green shell close to Shiny's brown one. She pointed with one leg. "Look, Shinola, you're starting to morph."

"I am? Where?"

"Right here."

And when Shiny stared really hard, she saw a little streak of jade emerging on one wing.

Impy waited for the mail each day. Sometimes Demo and Shiny were there too, but more often they were doing their jobs, so Impy was alone. When the landslide of letters poured through the slot onto the floor, he remembered how Demo used to hold both him and Shiny back, and so he waited a little longer, till the magazines crashed down. Then he scampered through the envelopes, searching for money. He didn't open any letters, but sometimes he found the telltale initial *R* in a return address: Gay *R* of America, National *R* Association of Stamp CollectoRs, Hip-hop *R*, The *R* Society for the PReservation of AmeRican Music. Impy wrote down the names of the senders, so he could tell Socra-Roach. He tried to guess how much money was inside each envelope.

Pops picked the mail up around noon. He too had learned to recognize the strange return addresses, and he usually opened those letters first. Often he'd count the money out loud: five hundred, six, seven, eight, nine hundred dollars. He'd stand and shake his head as if the world had just gone crazy.

One night, keeping watch on the office, Impy tried to do the math. Up until today the cash and checks had added up to about $3000. The gay roaches had sent $300, the stamp collectors $500, the hip-hop roaches $720.15, and the music preservationists another $1000. That brought the grand total to almost six thousand dollars, more than half of what Pops owed. Of course, *Pops* didn't know that, because he still hadn't realized that the *R* contributions were for him. Socra-Roach was going to do something about that, but he hadn't said what.

Despite the money in the drawer, Socra-Roach took nothing for granted. He asked all four branches of the community to make a list of their possessions. Once that was done, he asked the leaders to prioritize. "If we have to leave, we can't take everything," he pointed out. "So we need to figure out what's most important."

He had trouble getting the families to cooperate. Once they'd learned about the contributions, most of them had relaxed. The Harlequins were busy meditating on the proper path to take if they *should* have to move. The Green Banans were celebrating Shiny's safe return with songs and dances every night. The Maddies were practicing their hisses, in case they had to scare someone while they were on the road. And for the last two days, the Socras had reclined on their tiny couches and debated whether it would be better to pack their belongings in the morning or the afternoon. Socra-Roach was beside himself.

"Don't you understand this is a crisis?"

"There's money in Pops's drawer," someone answered.

"It may not be enough. We have to be prepared to leave, in case it's not."

"What is the meaning of prepared?" another listener asked innocently.

So then the Socras started talking about that. On his way back to the office, instead of tapping, Socra-Roach's walking stick seemed to jab against the floor.

CHAPTER FORTY-THREE

Preparations

TROY SAT IN HIS BEDROOM, his flute across his lap. He was worried. Each time he visited the club, he saw more things that needed to be done. Some of them were simple, like buying wineglasses for the party and cleaning out the junk in the storage area to make room for supplies. Someone needed to wax the floors. The freezer in the old refrigerator filled up with frost if it wasn't cleaned out every so often.

Troy raised the flute to his lips and started to play. His worries flew away. He played and played and played. By now he knew his practice songs by heart. He'd listened to flute music on his CD player and tried to figure out the melodies. He almost had his favorite tune down pat.

His folks were worried too. Their plans were complicated: work crews were to swoop in on the club at eight o'clock Sunday morning, as soon as Pops and Earlene had left. Charlie had hired painters and carpenters and bartenders and security guards. The KitKats had found a soundman to rig a better system and some spotlights. There were new doormats inscribed with *Pop's Corner* and a bright pink saxophone to be delivered, and bright tablecloths and big bouquets of flowers. All this work had to be done by seven thirty that night, when the benefit began.

Some things were going well. Earlene had figured out the food: deviled eggs from Mrs. Martin; fresh vegetables with dip, bowls of nuts, buffalo wings, little crab-cake sandwiches, and skewers of shrimp from the Korean takeout on the corner; and the local brewery had kicked in beer. The tickets had sold out quickly, and people who couldn't come had sent donations to the all-jazz radio station. The program managers had opened an account where they deposited both checks and cash. But there were also expenses—thousands of dollars' worth. Insurance on the building hadn't been paid, and there were cleaning and repairs that had to be done before the show.

Troy helped out all he could. One day he was washing the floor in the front hall when the mail arrived. Impy watched him sorting through the letters. A few of them looked interesting.

"Can I open your mail, Grandpa?" Troy shouted into the lounge.

"Is there anything from the bank?"

"No."

"Then go ahead."

Most of the envelopes were solicitations or credit card offers. But the last one was addressed not to *Resident* or *Box Holder* but to *Herbert Wiggins, Pop's Corner Jazz Club*. Troy didn't even glance at the return address. He ripped through the top of the envelope and reached inside. His fingers came back holding cash. He gasped.

"Grandpa! Come here!"

Pops was on a ladder dusting the photographs. "Just a minute . . ."

Troy counted the money: 50, 100, 150, 800. Eight hundred dollars. He looked for a letter explaining who had sent it, and why. There was nothing. He examined the envelope. In the upper left-hand corner, in tiny script, were these words: *BaRnum and Bailey's Pint-size CiRcus, 116 FRont Street, SaRasota, FloRida.*

"Grandpa!" Troy was thrilled. "You won't believe this! The circus sent you money!"

"What?" Pops climbed down the ladder and fished his reading glasses out of his shirt pocket. He peered at the envelope and shook his head in disgust. "This isn't for me. These *R* people think I'm someone else. I keep meaning to take their money to the police so they can send it back."

"But the envelope has your name and address, right here."

"I know that, Troy. But nobody sends money without an explanation." He handed the envelope, with the cash inside it, back to Troy. "Go put it in my top right-hand desk drawer. That's where I stuck the rest of them."

Troy put the money in the desk. He couldn't help noticing the other envelopes inside the drawer. Did they have money in them too? He peeked into one or two and saw the wads of cash inside. He read the return addresses. Like Grandpa'd said, the R's were all capitalized and in italics. Why in the world would anyone do that? Troy slipped the new envelope inside the rubber band with the others. It was then that he had an odd feeling. He looked at all the envelopes again. Most of them were typed, but there were two—today's and one other—that were handwritten. The script was elegant but tiny. Where have I seen something like that before? Troy asked himself. Then he remembered! That note Bitty had shown him . . . the one she'd said she'd found beside her pillow.

He went over the clues again. Money from groups all over the country . . . R's . . . miniature writing . . . the letter from the Louis Armstrong Institute . . . Shinola Banan . . .

Nothing added up.

CHAPTER FORTY-FOUR

Because of You

SOCRA-ROACH CALLED IMPY INTO HIS OFFICE.

"Last night I snuck inside the office building down the street and went online. I sent Aristotle an e-mail, asking how they'd heard we needed money. He wrote me back at once and said a Transient had wandered through the area, searching for your father. He wanted to find him because Petronovich's son was in trouble. The building where he lived in Baltimore would soon be sold at auction. The Transient mentioned Pop's Corner, and that made Aristotle think of me. So he met with his council, and they decided to send a check.

"What I want to know is, who sent a message to Petronovich?"

Impy hung his head. "Remember when I went outside and I got caught? I stuck a message for my dad on the base of a lamppost on Harford Road. I'd heard that lots of Transients go past there."

"What was in the message?"

Impy explained.

Socra-Roach stood with his mouth open. Then he burst out laughing. Laughter from Socra-Roach was so unusual that his young clerk came and stood in the doorway to make sure he was all right. Socra-Roach ignored him.

"So it's because of you," he spluttered.

"What do you mean?"

"The donations. Remember when I told you about our collective intelligence? Your message spread wherever Transients were going. When other roaches learned about our plight, they responded by sending checks and cash."

Now it was Impy's turn to be amazed. He pointed one foreleg at his chest. "Because of . . ."

"Because of you. Because you broke the rules and went outside to send a message to your father. Because of you, if all goes well"—here Socra-Roach hesitated—"*if* all goes well, we won't have to move, and neither will Pops and Earlene."

There was something else that Socra-Roach had learned online, but he didn't tell it to Impy or anyone else. Not yet. He'd gone to the bank's Web site to find out if the news of the foreclosure had been released. Instead he'd found this ad:

Celebrate Pop's Corner

Baltimore's longest-running jazz club needs a boost from its many longtime supporters.

Come and hear the
Queen of the Blues
and the King of Clarinet,
the All-Stars, the KitKats,
the Jinks, and more!

SUNDAY, AUGUST 9, at 7:30 p.m.
TICKETS $100

P.S.: Don't tell POPS!

Over the ad was stamped in bold black letters: **SOLD OUT**.

CHAPTER FORTY-FIVE

The Gift

TROY SAT IN HIS BEDROOM, his flute across his lap. Yesterday, the painters who were supposed to come to the club Sunday morning had canceled. Then his mom discovered that the oven in the bar's kitchen didn't work. "I'm afraid if I call a repairman, Pops will be suspicious," she'd told Troy. "He hasn't used that oven in ten years."

"What do we need it for, anyway?"

"To keep things hot. We have fifty pounds of ribs coming on Sunday afternoon. They'll need to be heated before they can be set out."

Troy flinched. "Mom, we only have five days left,

and there's so much that can go wrong."

His mother nodded. "I'm worried too. All we can do is hope for the best."

After the conversation, Troy had retreated to his room and done what seemed to help him most: practicing his flute. Last week he'd played a new song for his teacher. Afterward, she'd stared at him. "You have a gift," she'd said. "There are people who've studied the flute for years who can't play a melody like that." Troy had been pleased and flattered. Of course he'd practiced harder. *You have a gift.* . . . Suddenly he realized there was something he could do to make the party better. He went to the kitchen, where his mom was making salad.

"I want to play the flute at Grandpa's party," he said.

She looked surprised.

"Are you sure, Troy? There're going to be an awful lot of people there."

"I'm positive. I want to make the party special for Grandpa, no matter what."

His mom kissed him on the cheek. "Why don't you play for us when Charlie gets home? He's been working with the bands, so he knows what's on the program for that night."

Troy's dad came home late. He'd dropped by the club with a tray of chicken wings for his folks. Then Earlene had suggested that he eat with them. Pops wasn't so gracious.

"All of a sudden I see you and Zeena here each time I turn around. I've been running this club for almost fifty years. I ain't saying that I done a perfect job, but if there's something that you want to say to me, say it."

Earlene was mortified. "Herbert! That's no way to talk!"

"It's okay." Charlie grinned. "I realized I was out of touch, Dad, and I decided I wanted to spend more time with you."

"Don't start with that mushy stuff." Pops growled. Then, because he knew that he'd been rude, he pulled out a chair for Charlie. "Sit down, son, and help us polish off these wings," he said. "They sure do look good."

"That's why I'm home at eight instead of six," Charlie explained to his family. He took his necktie off and slumped down in his favorite chair.

Bitty jumped into his lap. "Tell me a story, Daddy."

"Not right now, Bitty. I'm beat."

Troy had already fetched his flute. Now, hearing how tired his dad was, he stepped back. But Zeena spoke for him.

"Troy wants to play for us."

"Me too," Bitty yammered.

"Quiet, hon. Right now we're listening to Troy."

႟

CHAPTER FORTY-SIX

Urgent Meeting!

IMPY, DEMO, AND SHINY stared at the sign. "What day is the meeting?" Impy asked. "And where? And at what time?"

"Shut up, Imp," Shiny said. "You know we're not invited."

"Not so." Carlita emerged from behind the radiator, carrying a bit of cracker in her mouth. She was so beautiful that Shiny couldn't help reaching out to touch her gold antennae ribbons.

"We don't have to go to the nursery?"

"Not this time. We'll be meeting behind the refrigerator today at three o'clock."

Carlita hurried on, her six legs dancing to an unheard beat.

* * *

The coils of the refrigerator were packed. Socra-Roach stood on the wood chip that served as his podium. He called the meeting to order with a reading from Tagore, a roach poet of ancient India. Then he waved his walking stick cheerfully.

"I bring good news!" he said.

"*Good* news?" The words echoed through the crowd.

"*Good* news," Socra-Roach repeated.

And he told them about the party. Everyone clapped and cheered. The Green Banans proposed a celebration. "Let's put on our dancing shoes," they yelled.

"That's exactly why I want to talk with you." Socra-Roach waited for silence. He tapped his walking stick on the podium for emphasis. "We're not going to Pops's party—not a single one of us."

"*Why not?*" Whining and wheedling began. Socra-Roach stood firm.

"If the guests see us, they'll get upset. This is a fancy event, and to them we're just a bunch of dirty pests."

"But this is the biggest celebration the club has ever had. We shouldn't have to hide!"

"Try to be rational. Think about the long-term consequences of your actions, instead of what will make you happy for one night."

"He's right." Carlita came to stand by Socra-Roach's side. "And furthermore, I promise you that once Pops's bills are paid, we'll have a party of our own—the biggest ever."

"With music?"

"With live roach bands and pizza and soda pop and

strobe lights and lovely paper umbrellas. We'll stay up all day and all night, even the nymphs."

"But what if"—the voice was small and frail—"something bad happens this Sunday? What if the party doesn't make enough money?"

All the roaches turned and stared at the tiny nymph who'd dared to ask these questions. He was a little Socra with a nervous face.

Socra-Roach nodded at him. His tone was grave. "It is *possible*—not likely, but *possible*—that the benefit will fail. If it does, we have a set of emergency plans. They aren't perfect, but they will keep us safe and together until we make more permanent decisions."

"Who's going to guard the money in Pops's office?" Impy asked.

"Nobody. Every single one of us will be downstairs."

"But what if someone—"

"No exceptions."

Shiny leaned over to Impy. "Don't be a worrywart," she whispered. "Everything is going to turn out fine."

༄

CHAPTER FORTY-SEVEN

No Mistake

"WHAT'S THIS?" Pops asked out loud. There was an index card propped on his cluttered desk. He had just sat down in his office to write a check. It was late Saturday afternoon, and he'd finished setting up for the two bands that would play that night. Now he took his reading glasses out of his shirt pocket and perched them on his nose. Even so, it was hard for him to read the tiny script.

Dear Mr. Wiggins,

This letter is to inform you that the contributions you have received in the mail with the following return addresses are in fact donations to Pop's

*Corner and **were not** sent to you by accident or mistake. They come from jazz fans all over the country, and from others who have learned of your generosity over many years. . . .*

"Wait a minute," Pops said. He stubbed out his cigar. He reached up to the ledge over his desk and took down the magnifying glass he used to look up telephone numbers. He started reading the card again.

Dear Mr. Wiggins:
    *This letter is to inform you that the contributions you have received in the mail with the following return addresses are in fact donations to Pop's Corner and **were not** sent to you by accident or mistake. They have come from jazz fans . . .*

Pops scanned to the bottom of the card. There were the names of organizations, neatly printed:

> *Boston* R *Society of the ARts*
> *BPO*R
> *BS*R *of AmeRica*
> *DemocRatic Association of* R

The whole list was there, except for the one that had come yesterday from the circus. Perhaps whoever had written this note had not known about it.

Pops read the letter one more time, slowly, saying each word out loud, to be sure there was nothing he was missing. **The money is for you,** it said in darkened script. And it was signed, *Friends of Pops and Earlene's.* Who were these friends? Why hadn't they come and told him they had money to offer? And why was their writing so tiny?

Today's mail lay piled by the front door. Pops brought the whole stack back inside his office. He went through the pile of papers one by one: flyers, solicitations, but there in the middle was another envelope: *Big Hat Jazz-R-Cize, 2334 Poole St., Houston, Texas.* Pops tore it open. Enclosed was a check for two thousand dollars, made out to him. Most of the check was in computer script, but in the right-hand corner was a tiny signature: *Artesina Cucarracha.* Pops's hands trembled. He looked through the last few pieces of mail, and at the bottom found what he thought might be another of the strange letters. But this one was different. It had no return address and was made out to *Impetuous R., Pop's Corner, 116 Washington Street, Baltimore, Maryland. Impetuous R.?* Who in the world was he? Pops ripped the letter open.

My dearest son,

    I got your message and I'm sympathetic. I don't have any money to send you for the jazz club because I believe money is the tool of greedy capitalists. Impetuous, wherever you and your mother and the rest of the family end up, remember this slogan: Workers of the World, Unite! Only by acting together will we be able to throw off the yoke of capitalism forever.

    Your loving father,

    PetRonovich

P.S. I hope you find a solution that lets you stay at Pop's Corner. It's a lovely place.

Pops reread the letter, this time out loud. This was the craziest thing yet! He'd never heard of someone called Impetuous. Nobody lived at Pop's Corner but him and Earlene. Yet, in a strange way, the letter confirmed what the index card had said: that for some reason, groups were sending money to keep the club going. The money *was* for him after all.

He added it up. $8,342.15. Not all that he needed, but a lot. I should deposit it right now, Pops thought. But when he checked his pocket watch, he saw that the bank was closed. He could deposit it in the ATM—but the idea of dropping all that money into a metal slot made him nervous. He was so confused and excited he could hardly think. Should he tell Earlene? He wasn't sure.

Impy watched as Pops stood up. There was a spring to his step, and before the door had closed, Impy could hear whistling from the other side. "Mood Indigo," a Duke Ellington classic. But the way Pops was whistling, the song should have been called "Mood Joy." Impy wished that he could whistle too.

My dearest son, the note had said. And at the end, *Your loving father*. How wonderful—wonderful!—to know that you were loved.

CHAPTER FORTY-EIGHT

A Very Special Roach

AFTER HE HEARD POPS READ the letter from his father, Impy ran home and told his mom. She was surprised and pleased, partly to hear that a letter had come but also because Impy was so happy. "What did the letter say?" she asked.

"I'm not too sure . . . Something about workers of the world . . ."

"Oh, yes." His mother smiled. "That was his path."

"He loves me! At the front he wrote, *My dearest son*, and he signed it, *Your loving father*."

His mother smiled again. "He is a very special roach," she said.

For a little while Impy forgot about being a secret agent. Then he remembered and realized he'd left Pops's office with no one keeping watch.

"I have to go," he said.

"Where?"

"I have a job. Socra-Roach gave it to me. It's very important."

"Then maybe you'd better." His mother sighed. "You boys," she said. "Always running off to do something more important than stay home."

"I'll be back," Impy said. "I'm just downstairs."

"Go," she said, laughing.

CHAPTER FORTY-NINE

᠗᠍᠍᠍᠍᠍᠍᠍᠍᠍᠍᠍᠍᠍᠍᠍᠍᠍᠍᠍᠍᠍᠍᠍᠍᠍᠍᠍᠍

Jealous

NO JAZZ GREAT EVER PLAYED THE FLUTE, Pops had told him. Troy was sure that wasn't true. He practiced more. His parents couldn't believe how well he played. He was gaining confidence. There was only one problem: Bitty.

Bitty was jealous. Why should Troy get to play at the party when Bitty had to stand on the sidelines watching? Wouldn't the guests want to see her perform, too?

Her mom and dad said no. So did Troy. Bitty threw a tantrum. She refused to eat. She refused to take a bath or brush her teeth. "It's not fair!" she yelled.

She snuck into Troy's room when he was practicing.

"Look at me, Troy!" she cried, pirouetting around the bed.

"Bitty, go away."

"I made up a song and dance. It's called 'Pop's Corner Special.'" Bitty sang some of the lyrics and danced along:

"My grandpa is so special.
Everybody calls him Pops.
He runs a famous jazz club
And cleans it with a mop.
It's the Pop's Corner Special,
Playing music all the time. . . ."

Troy rolled his eyes. "Would you please go away?" he said.

"You're so mean!"

Bitty ran out and slammed the door behind her. She was so mad she couldn't even shout. She threw herself down on her bed. She would be a star, she promised herself, no matter what Troy said.

༄༅

CHAPTER FIFTY

Fourteen Hours Left, and Counting . . .

POPS GOT UP AT FIVE O'CLOCK on Sunday morning
and made a pot of coffee. Then, instead of slipping on his
usual baggy pants, striped shirt, and brown fedora, he
dressed in his old blue suit. He looked through his neckties
and found one that was especially nice. They didn't wear the
wide kind anymore, Charlie had told him several years ago,
but he couldn't care less what other men were wearing. There
was only one person he wanted to impress: Earlene.

She was still asleep. He sat down on the easy chair beside
the bed. The money in the drawer preyed on his mind. Was
what the card said true? He went through the same old

arguments: *No one sends money to people they don't know.*

But the letters were addressed to you, his mind countered. And someone had written the index card, too, and put it on his desk.

That part bothered him especially. He and Charlie were the only ones who had keys to the club. How had the person with the card come in? How had he known where to find Pops's desk? Why was his writing so tiny? While the coffee was brewing, Pops had tried to write that small. No matter how he cramped his hand, he couldn't do it. And why would someone *want* to, anyway?

Pops sat back in his chair and closed his eyes. Jumbled memories ran through his mind: he and Earlene on their knees, scrubbing the floor the day before the club had opened; staying up all night to deep-fry chicken, grate cabbage for coleslaw, make sheets of dinner rolls. How nervous they had been back then. Even though they had big stars to sing on opening night, they couldn't quite believe anyone would show up. But they'd come, and Pops and Earlene had worked all night, discovering what they needed the hard way, running from the kitchen to the bar and back again, collapsing, exhausted, after the last customer had left. They'd fallen asleep in their clothes because they were too tired to take them off. But sometime in the night, Earlene had reached over to hold his hand. "We did it, Herbert," she'd whispered.

There'd been hard times: the fire, the months when nearby streets were closed while the city was digging the subway, the nights when big acts canceled and the ticket money had to be refunded. Somehow, the club had always survived.

Earlene stirred in the bed. She was breathing peacefully, her white hair spread out on her pillow, her face lined with wrinkles—like his. So many years . . . Pops sighed. Joys, disappointments, hard work, and now they were old. But there was still time for love.

She opened her eyes as he was sitting there. "Herbert—you're already dressed. You should have woken me up."

"I'll get you some coffee."

"My goodness, I'm late. We have to leave here by eight."

"I don't see what the hurry is," Pops said gruffly. But of course he didn't mean it; he would do every single thing he could to make this day a special one.

CHAPTER FIFTY-ONE

Makeover

THE WORKERS, WHO'D BEEN HIDING down the block until Pops's truck turned the corner, charged the club. Charlie gave orders like a marine commander: "Painters and deliverymen, this side. Repairmen, follow me. Decorators, this is my wife, Zeena. She'll tell you where to start."

Troy was the errand boy. He knew where everything was stored, so when someone needed an extension cord or a roll of paper towels or a broom, he could fetch it right away. Bitty tagged along behind. She was still whining about the show.

"I want to be a rock star too."

"I'm not a rock star. Anyway, I thought you were handing out programs."

"Rock stars don't hand out programs."

"Bitty, look at me. I'm carrying a bucket and a mop. Do you think rock stars do that?"

"It's not fair." Bitty stuck out her lower lip.

Troy decided to ignore her. For a moment he stood still and watched the transformation: the back wall of the lounge was turning a soft yellow. Two women had covered the old tables with creamy green cloths. Vases of roses topped the old piano and the bar. Pops's ancient sound system was being carted out piece by piece, to be replaced by a modern one. Deliveries poured in through the back door: platters of food, cases of beer and wine. Things were happening so fast that when Troy looked the

other way, he didn't know what he'd see when he turned back.

Impy kept watch on the office. Charlie ran in and out, writing checks and collecting receipts. Then Troy came in alone. Charlie must have sent him to get something, because he scoured the desktop until he found the rubber stamp with the club's name and address on it.

Parting the sea of papers and envelopes, his hand fell on the index card. He stared at the tiny script. Then he read it. When he came to the signature—*Friends of Pops and Earlene's*—he gasped.

"Dad!"

"Troy, where's that business stamp?"

"I . . . I—" Troy glanced down and saw the stamp resting in his right hand. "I'm bringing it. But . . ."

The soundman was waiting outside the door with Charlie, tapping his foot. Troy knew his discovery would have to wait.

Impy saw the whole thing. He remembered the day that Troy had opened the letter from the pint-size circus—how excited he'd been. He'd thumbed through the rest of the envelopes too, examining the return addresses with curiosity. Impy wondered whether Troy liked mysteries, and whether *he'd* ever thought about being a secret agent. It would be fun to have a human partner. Impy imagined the two of them dressed in dark suits, wearing sunglasses to hide their identities. Troy would look for the big clues, and Impy would search for the small ones: a tiny drop of ink, or a cracker crumb, or a hair on the carpet. He pictured the glass door of their office, imprinted with black letters:

> Troy Allen Wiggins, FBI
> Impetuous Roach, FBI

But there was something not quite right about that image. Impy thought harder. Now he had it:

> Troy Allen Wiggins, FBI
> Impetuous Roach, FB*R*I

He grinned. With a title like that, no one would call him *runt* or *mutt* or *worrywart* ever again.

CHAPTER FIFTY-TWO

"Pay in Full"

POPS COULDN'T EAT ONE MORE BITE. He watched as Earlene nibbled at a buckwheat cake. Her color was good this morning, and the red hat she was wearing made her white hair gleam. She had clapped and sung all the way through the church service, talked with old friends and the minister as if she'd seen them just last week. Pops had hung back, praying that no one had heard the news about the club. But if they had, nobody mentioned it to Earlene. He'd found a chair for her to sit in during the social hour, but even so he worried that she'd be worn out before they left. Sure enough, she'd nodded off inside the truck. When she woke up, Pops asked, "Are you sure you want pancakes? We could go home, so you could rest, and then come back."

"Of course I want pancakes." Earlene was adamant. So here they were, in the booth at IHOP. Pops didn't have the appetite he'd had when he was young, but he managed to put away a plate of bacon, eggs, and sausage, with a side of hotcakes, too.

It was too early for the movie when they got back in the truck. Earlene tipped back her seat to take a snooze, and Pops turned on the radio. Earlene turned it off. "It's hard for me to nap with the radio on," she said.

"But it's always on at home. That is, it was until Charlie took it. He hasn't said a word about bringing it back, either."

So Pops sat there and watched as Earlene fell asleep. All last night and this morning he'd been calculating. He didn't have enough to pay the bills, but he was close. If only every single one didn't include the message *Pay in Full.*

CHAPTER FIFTY-THREE

The Heist

DO-ZEN REFUSED to go to the basement. Demo argued and pleaded, but the elder shook his head. "I'd rather stay here," he said tartly.

Demo tried to explain. "People . . . give . . . money . . . roaches . . . hide."

Do-zen didn't understand. "I'd be delighted if you stayed, my lad. And I know a lovely place where we can rest."

"Nope."

"Come with me," Do-zen said. He left the men's room wall and crawled into the office. Demo could see the last roaches hurrying downstairs. He wondered if he should yell to them and ask for help. But at times someone else's pleading made Do-zen all the more stubborn. Demo followed him into the office and up the wall. He climbed out on the ledge that stood above the desk. Pops's magnifying glass was lying there. Do-zen looked through it.

"Pemo, finally I can see your handsome face. How I wish I had a little glass like this to carry with me on my travels. Then I could have seen the Creepie boss up close."

He settled down for a nap. Demo sat beside him.

"What was her name, my lad?"

"Czarina Pepina."

"That's right—Cornelia Pepperstick. What a charming creature, don't you think?"

Demo shrugged. He wasn't interested in girls except as friends. Czarina had been lively, though. Demo tried to remember their last conversation. Something about it made him uneasy. What *was* it she had said to him?

Do-zen's mind had fixed on something new. "I learned some songs in England years ago," he said. "They were written by a roach group called The Beetles. My favorite had a chorus that went like this: *We all live in a yellow bugmobile, a yellow bugmobile, a yellow . . .*" Demo looked over. He saw the elder's eyes starting to close. Maybe he'd sleep through the whole party. That would be good—the more still they stayed, the less chance that they'd be seen. Even so, Demo vowed to keep himself awake.

The room was warm and bright. Do-zen was snoring softly. Demo felt his eyes drift shut. He opened them— there. He was awake, wasn't he? Wasn't he?

Most people are nice, Troy's parents always said, but that doesn't mean that *everyone* is nice. Even though you'd like to trust every single person you meet, the truth is that you can't. Troy knew that well enough. After all, anyone who watched the news had seen murderers and con artists and petty thieves. But today was just so busy: people he'd never seen before were running in and out, bringing things, taking things away, going into all the rooms on the first floor to paint or change the wiring or simply vacuum the floor. So when two young men came in claiming to be part of the cleaning crew, Troy had no reason to doubt them.

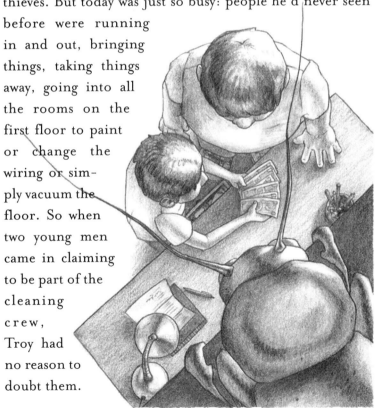

By the time Demo woke up, the men were in the office, and the door was closed. He lay on the ledge observing them. One was thin and wiry, and the other tall and fat. Both were dressed in clean white T-shirts. They must be part of the work crew, Demo thought. He watched as they searched the top of the desk. "It's not here, Sam," the thin one said.

"I'll check the walls," Sam answered.

"Look behind those photographs. There might be something hidden there."

One by one they came down: John Coltrane, Nat King Cole, Thelonious Monk. But there was nothing behind them except dust.

Demo stared. Why were they looking behind the pictures?

"How about that file cabinet?"

The thin man rifled through it. "I don't see a thing."

"George told my aunt he'd brought more of those envelopes this week."

Those envelopes—suddenly Demo understood. In the very same second he remembered the words Czarina Pepina had said to him: "A plan's afoot to rip Pops off." A chill ran through him. He hadn't really understood the warning, but he should have told somebody anyway. The right-hand drawer was open now. The thin man poked among the letters, pulled one out. A wad of cash peeked from the envelope. "Harry, take a look at this."

"Oh, *yes*—"

Here was the money from the fitness club in Houston.

Next came the contributions from the democrats, and the scouts, and the fine arts council.

"This one's a check."

"Take it anyway."

More and more money piled on the desktop, precious dollars that might have saved the club and let Earlene live out her life at home, where she wanted to be.

❧

CHAPTER FIFTY-FOUR

The Motion Picture Show

POPS HADN'T BEEN TO THE MOVIES in at least ten years. Earlene had, but only a few times, and those were with her girlfriends. Pops swung the old truck into the downtown parking lot. "That'll be two dollars," the attendant said.

"Two dollars for a square of asphalt?"

"Yes, sir."

"There's no one else here."

"Two dollars, sir."

Pops grunted. It wasn't the boy's fault, he knew that; but in his mind, two dollars should have paid for the motion pictures and the popcorn, too. He pulled into space number fourteen and put on the brake. Earlene was still asleep. He put his hand on her shoulder.

"We're here, honey."

"Where?"

"At the movies."

She took a minute to wake up. "I'm so excited. Let me find those tickets Zeena gave me . . . Here they are."

"What're we watching?"

"The first one's about Ray Charles. I'm not sure about the second one."

"You sure you want to see *two* movies?"

"I've never been surer in my life."

Pops went around and opened the truck door. He held out his hand. Young guys didn't know what it meant to be a gentleman, but Pops had grown up in a better time. Earlene climbed down. They went inside the theater. When Pops saw the price of popcorn he almost died; but then he remembered his vow to make his wife as happy as he possibly could. He went with her to find a pair of seats, then circled back and got the giant soda and the tub of popcorn. He bought a little box of mints—she'd always liked those—and took it all back to their seats.

"Herbert, how nice." Earlene took a sip of soda. They watched the previews, and the feature started. Pops had met Ray Charles, and he didn't think the actor looked too much like him, but the story was good. He glanced over at Earlene. She was smiling, but he could tell by her breathing that she'd gone back to sleep. Pops shook his head. He'd told her that they'd planned too much to do; they should have gone to church one day and the movies the next. But Earlene was stubborn. Once she fixed on an idea, it was hard to change her mind. Pops sighed. He sat back in his chair and enjoyed the rest of the motion picture.

Earlene woke up when it was almost over. "Oh, my," she said. "I think I missed something."

༄

CHAPTER FIFTY-FIVE

Stage Fright

TROY STOOD IN THE CORNER of the storeroom, his flute in his hands. This space was quiet now. In the lounge, workers were putting the final touches on the newly built stage. Spotlights were hanging from a scaffolding. Neighbors worked in the kitchen, baking biscuits and heating ribs in the newly fixed oven. It seemed like everything and everyone was doing well.

Except for Troy. His heart was banging and his mouth felt dry. When he put the flute to his lips, there was hardly enough breath to play a single note. He'd drunk a little water, but it hadn't helped that much. The program had everything it needed. Why in the world had he said he wanted to play too?

He could back out, of course. He could go to his dad right now and say he'd changed his mind. Charlie would simply tell the guests there'd been a program change. No one would be the worse for it.

He took a deep breath and raised the flute back to his lips.

CHAPTER FIFTY-SIX

The Leap

THE ROBBERS WERE CRACKING UP. By now they'd jammed Pops's desk chair in front of the door to wedge it closed. They were emptying the envelopes and putting the money into their pockets.

"Miami Beach, here we come." The fat one chuckled.

"And Disney World. I've always wanted to go there."

Demo stood on the ledge above them, watching. Dozen had awakened. At first he'd been confused, but then he looked through the magnifying glass and figured out what was going on.

"Demo, they're taking Pops's money!"

Demo just stood there. He imagined a line of roaches dragging their belongings out the basement window and onto the sidewalk; Pops and Earlene slowly climbing into his old truck, with their furniture piled into the back; the building's new owner ordering his workers to take down the neon saxophone sign and throw it out. He—Demo—could have changed all that. He could have gone to Socra-Roach and told him about meeting the Creepies. He could have thought, It doesn't matter if I get into trouble. It might have been hard, but he could have figured out the words to tell the others of Czarina's warning.

Below him the men worked steadily, their hairy heads bobbing with each motion.

Demo had an idea.

He was scared.

He jumped.

The fall felt like slow motion. He landed in a thatch of hair. The thief didn't even notice he was there. Demo ran down the fat man's neck and dove into the space between his collar and his back.

It took the man a second to react. He cursed and started flailing at his back. Demo escaped the blows by running down his spine.

"What's *wrong* with you?"

"I've got a bug inside my shirt."

"For heaven's sake . . ." But then the other thief stopped dead. "What is this? I've got one on me too." He ripped his T-shirt off. A roach was crouched between his shoulder blades. If you'd looked hard enough, you would have seen that it was wearing tiny spectacles.

"Get it off me, dude."

"*Take the money and run!*"

"*Hold on!*" The fat man smacked his side. A bug fell to the floor. He lifted his heavy boot and stomped. Then he pulled Pops's desk chair to one side. The door was opening on its own.

"What's going on in here? I heard shouting. . . ."

"RUN, YOU IDIOT!"

But the security guard had already pulled his gun.

CHAPTER FIFTY-SEVEN

Pops's Secret

TROY'S FATHER WATCHED WHILE the paddy wagon drove away with the two robbers locked inside. Then he went back into the office. He stared at the money the men had sheepishly pulled from their pockets.

Where had it come from? Why hadn't Pops told him it was here?

As soon as he'd counted the cash and checks and locked them in the safe behind the bar, he told Zeena what he'd found. She was astounded. "Eight thousand dollars? Could Pops have won the lottery?"

"Who knows? I never realized he had so many secrets."

"Do you think Earlene knew?"

"No way. She was worried that they might not have enough cash to pay for breakfast."

"I hope she's doing okay. She promised me she'd sleep if she got—"

"Dad! Mom!" Troy came racing from the club's front door, with Bitty behind him. "Four limousines are pulling up outside!"

"Four limousines!" Bitty echoed.

"I'm coming," Charlie said.

CHAPTER FIFTY-EIGHT

"He were brave, for a geezer."

"WAKE UP, BIRDBRAIN," somebody said. "You think we got all night?"

Demo blinked. He knew that he was dead. The last thing he remembered was the sole of a huge boot headed down on top of him.

The roach above him wore his hat pulled low. "Say a prayer to Vibram soles, my dude. Your shell got stuck a-tween the threads. When the cager hopped into the paddy wagon, you fell out. The others seen and toted you inside."

"Inside where?"

"Look around you, bro. Ain't you never seen this spot afore?"

Demo looked. The place where he was lying looked curiously like the loose panel in the ceiling of the front hall closet. There were several roaches gathered around him, all wearing hats. Could there be Creepies in heaven, too?

"You was lucky," the Creepie said. "We thought you was gone. How'd you get stuck inside the bad boy's boot?"

"I fell."

"The geezer did the same. He dropped off of the other cager's back, into the street. By the time us got there, he were dead."

Demo started crying. A small, broad-shouldered roach was watching him, wide-eyed.

"We never cry, because we's mean and tough."

"Be quiet, Shorty. This bug just lost his gramps. We need somebody from this dude's home gang. Thuggy, scoot down to the cellar and bring a chica back."

"Not Shorty. Buttkicker. I changed my handle, Axel. Did you forget?"

"I just might have, Buttkicker. Sorry 'bout that."

In a moment Demo saw Carlita looking down at him. Thuggy must have told her what had happened. She wiped the tears from Demo's eyes and helped him to his feet.

"Us gotta bounce, my sweet. Birdbrain, we's sorry 'bout your pal. Him were brave, for a geezer. You was too. Youse two roaches freaked them bad boys out."

The Creepies hurried away.

❦

CHAPTER FIFTY-NINE

The Face of Reality

EARLENE SLEPT THROUGH the second movie, too. Again Pops had offered to take her home so she could rest in her own bed. She refused. "We've got free seats," she pointed out.

"But if you get too tired—"

"I'll let you know."

"Earlene." Pops shook his head. He knew he might as well give up.

The second picture was about a soldier trying to get home from the war. Pops had been in the Korean War, but he'd never gone to the front lines. He hadn't cared for army life: up at dawn, marching, saluting, taking orders. He didn't want to get his brains blown out for arguments he didn't understand. But he was lucky. He never got hurt, and when the train pulled into Baltimore and he saw Earlene from the window, waiting for him on the platform, he vowed he'd never go away again.

She'd run the club all by herself while he was gone and done a good job, too The acts were booked for the next six months, and all the bills were paid. The bills . . . Would Mr. Foley take the partial payment? It killed Pops not to know. Tomorrow, he and Earlene could be packing. Even so, he was glad he hadn't told her. What good would it have done to make her suffer even one day longer than she had to?

The movie ended. Pops hadn't even noticed most of what was going on. The lights came on and the audience got up to leave. Earlene woke up and smiled. She glanced at her watch.

"Seven—that's good."

"What's good?"

"That's just the time I wanted to go home."

Pops tried to hide his exasperation. "You slept through two movies. We could have been home hours ago. You could have napped in your own bed."

"No, I wanted to be here, with you." She took his arm. "It's been a very special day."

As he started the truck, Pops realized that he didn't want to go home, either. All day they'd avoided the ugly face of reality. Now they were about to bump smack up against it. *Pay in Full*, the letters said. Pops swallowed.

When he saw the limousines in front of the club, his first thought was that the building had been sold while he and Earlene were gone. A lump rose in his throat. He couldn't speak.

But Earlene was smiling. Pops looked again. There was Charlie standing in the door. Why was he wearing a tuxedo? And the woman beside him, the one in the evening gown. . . .

"It can't be."

"Yes, it can."

Time slowed down. Pops started noticing weird things: the sign with the pink saxophone was blowing neon bubbles, which it hadn't done in years, and all the missing lights in the marquee had been replaced. There was a silky banner over the door: CELEBRATE BALTIMORE'S OLDEST JAZZ CLUB. And people—dressed-up people—were coming from every direction.

"Park your car, sir?" The young man dressed in a blue uniform was smiling at him through the truck window.

"I—I—"

"Yes, thank you." Earlene reached over and took Pops's hand. "Let's go inside," she said, "and see what's happening."

CHAPTER SIXTY

The Best Party of All

THE GUESTS HAD FORMED a pathway when they learned the old truck had arrived. They stood on either side, applauding as Pops and Earlene came in. Old friends— musicians from twenty, thirty, fifty years ago—were standing together, grinning and waving. "SURPRISE!" they shouted. Pops's mouth dropped open in amazement, but he snapped it shut. Earlene smiled up at him. He realized suddenly why they'd spent the day outside the club. *"You knew about this,"* he mouthed.

"We had to get you out of here so they could fix it up."

"It looked all right before," Pops pretended to grump.

But he kept sneaking nervous glances at the brand-new stage, the sound system, the tablecloths, the flowers.

"Who paid for this?" he whispered to his wife.

"They charged a hundred dollars for each ticket. After they sold out, other donors came through, too. People sent checks from all across the country."

"How could they have known?"

"Jazz stations talked about the party every hour, just before the news came on. That's why we had to take your radio away."

"But, Earlene . . ." Pops looked down into her lovely face. He wondered if she knew how much they owed. It might take more than just a party to pay that off.

Then he remembered the envelopes in the right-hand drawer. There were thousands of dollars Earlene didn't even know about. He took her face in his hands. She seemed to understand. "Herbert," she whispered. "Everything is going to be just fine."

The two of them sat in a pair of easy chairs beside the stage. Pops didn't know whether to laugh or cry. He felt a light inside him grow stronger and brighter. His dark fears, so ever-present in the last few weeks, were fading, and joy had taken root instead.

"Herbie, do you remember me?"

The woman wore a bright red evening gown. Diamonds glittered on her neck and wrist. Pops thought fast.

"This was the second club you played in, wasn't it? Before you got the contract with Atlantic?"

"In fact, that night they were here watching me. I'll never forget this place. And it looks wonderful."

"Uhhh . . . thanks."

"I think of you often. If you hadn't let me sing, I might not be where I am right now."

She hugged him and moved on.

That scene was repeated many times. Bitty, proud in her new blue dress, had sat down on Pops's lap. She was sure that all the guests had come to meet her too: famous stars and not-so-famous ones, musicians from the symphony, the opera, dinner clubs, and jams in someone's basement or garage. The KitKats, who'd helped organize the benefit, shook hands with Pops. Jazz fans had come from Washington, D.C., and Philadelphia. Pops's old waitstaff were here, squeezed into uniforms they'd outgrown twenty years ago. And there were the neighbors, dressed in their Sunday best. "We were so worried for you, Pops," one of them whispered. "We know Earlene's bad off. We told that to the man who claimed he was going to buy this place. He didn't even blink."

"He won't be back," Pops said.

The evening had been a blur. There was wonderful music, of course, and then a moment when the crowd was chanting "*Speech!*"

Later, Pops couldn't remember what he'd said. Earlene claimed it had been something like this: *Long ago, when we opened this joint , we didn't know if we would make it; but we did know we loved music, and we wanted other people to have the chance to hear it too. Music has changed, and so have we.*

Pops had gestured to himself. He'd been tall and strong when he was young, but now his suit hung loose around his frame.

We don't always agree about what's good: Earlene has her favorites, and so do I. But we do agree that everyone deserves the chance to show an audience what they can do.

One moment stopped Pops in his tracks. That was when—sometime in the middle of the program—Troy stepped up on the stage. Pops could see that he was scared. But Troy looked straight at him.

"This is for you," he'd said quietly. He lifted the flute to his lips and started playing. His fingers danced. Notes—a whole tuneful of notes—lifted up and flew around the room. The listeners held their breath. The music was flowing water, pigeons soaring in the city sky, ferns on the hillside.

Bitty watched and listened. She didn't like the way the audience was watching Troy instead of her. Her feet began to itch. *No, Bitty,* she told herself, but her other half said *Yes!* She jumped off Grandpa's lap, darted in front of Troy, and starting dancing "Pop's Corner Special." She was doing great, she thought, twirling in her new blue dress, but Troy looked mad. He played faster. She danced faster. Then her mother's arms descended from behind and yanked her off the stage. By the time the audience had finished applauding, Bitty was stuck in the apartment, yowling, with the door closed tight.

Troy was so mad that he could hardly listen to the clapping and cheering. Pops came up and hugged him. Troy let his nervous body relax into his grandpa's. He was coming down to earth after a wild flight. It felt good to breathe again.

And later, one of the old musicians, hobbling on his

cane, found Troy in the crowded room. "Can I see your flute?" he asked.

"It's really my teacher's," Troy explained. He opened the case and got it out. The old man took it in his hands. He played Troy's song from memory; and after he'd gone through it once, he played a part of it again. "Right here," he said. "This bit. Do you remember how you slurred those notes?"

"I think so."

"Did someone teach you that?"

"No, I just like the way it sounds."

"Uh-huh . . ." The old man played the part again. "It took me a while to figure that out," he said. "We were in New Orleans with Cab Calloway. He put me on the flute, which I didn't usually play. So I had to work at it." He picked Troy's flute back up. "Later I added this—" He played a trill that was like nothing Troy had ever heard. He showed Troy how he did it. "This way."

"Like this?"

"That's a start . . . Here."

He showed him once again.

"You're going to be good," he said, before he walked away.

CHAPTER SIXTY-ONE

෧෨

What Socra-Roach Really Meant

"IT'S ALMOST OVER," Shiny said. "And I've hardly heard a thing. In an hour or so, all that great music will be gone."

"I know," Impy sighed. The time in the basement had been a letdown. Socra-Roach had set up a series of lectures for the entertainment and education of the community, but topics like Classic Roach Poetry and The History of Roaches During the Mesozoic Era didn't capture Impy's or Shiny's interest. The program for nymphs, How to Grow Up to Be the Best Cockroach You Can Be, didn't draw them either. When Carlita came in halfway through the evening with Demo, she'd shooed them both away. Now they were bored.

"Maybe . . ." Shiny whispered.

Impy knew he shouldn't ask. "Maybe what?"

"Maybe if we went to the apartment . . . I mean, nobody's there, because they're all at the party."

"If we went to the apartment, what?"

"We could hear the music better."

"We're supposed to stay here," Impy pointed out.

"Shut up, Imp. What Socra-Roach really meant to say was, *Don't let anyone see you.* That's what he was worried about."

"That's true."

"But who will see us if we climb up through the wall? We won't even poke our heads out till we get to the apartment. That way we'll be doing what Socra-Roach wants us to—staying hidden."

Shiny seemed pleased with herself. She examined her purple antennae ribbon intently. "If we hide behind the washer, and then crawl up the pipe on the far side, we can climb all the way to Pops and Earlene's bathroom . . ."

Before she'd finished speaking, she and Impy were scuttling toward the laundry room.

❧

CHAPTER SIXTY-TWO

The Note

"NO FAIR!" BITTY SOBBED. "The party wasn't over. I didn't even get a cookie!"

She was lying on Pops and Earlene's bed, kicking her feet in the air. The skirt of her blue dress flipped up and down. Bitty looked at the closed door that led downstairs. She almost never got a spanking, but she had a bad feeling about opening that door. She kicked her feet and yelled some more.

After a while she quieted down, because the music was so loud no one could hear her anyway. She stuck her lower lip out in a pout. "They liked the way I danced," she argued to herself. She got up and started dancing, singing the melody that Troy had played. Then Troy came upstairs too. Bitty ran and hid. But for some reason he wasn't angry anymore, so she came back out.

"Play that song again," she begged. Troy did, enjoying himself because there was no reason to be nervous. Bitty danced. "I'll be very famous," she said after the tune was over, "and you can work for me."

"Maybe you'll work for me."

"Maybe." Bitty looked around the room, trying to decide what to do next. The TV was there, of course, but she'd watched TV so many times . . . Then she thought of something.

"Want to see where my bug lives?"

Troy shrugged.

"Bring your flute," Bitty said.

They went into the bathroom. Bitty pointed out a little crack down near the bottom of the paneling. "Play now."

Troy did. For a moment, nothing happened. Then a roach darted out of the opening, onto the wall. Troy's eyes almost popped. For a split second the bug actually seemed to be doing the samba! But before he could get a really good look, a smaller roach appeared. It grabbed the first one and yanked it back inside the crack.

"That was her!" Bitty yelled. "Did you see her, Troy? That was her!"

"That was a roach."

"It was my bug! She loves music, just like me!"

"A roach." Troy repeated in disgust. Something occurred to him then—something weird. He remembered the letters with the tiny script, and the envelopes, and the return addresses marked with capital R's. Those roaches lived here too. Grandma always yelled when she caught sight of one, but he'd seen plenty: on the basement ceiling, or running along the crack in the downstairs bathroom wall. There were whole families of them. When he told Grandpa, he always said the same thing: "Tomorrow I'll get some bug spray." Could the R letters have something to do with the roaches? No. Troy shook his head. It was impossible.

"She came home in my purse," Bitty went on. "But at night I let her sleep inside my dollhouse. We both danced. Then Mom tried to murder her, so I had to bring her back here. But she left the note! Remember the note, Troy?"

"What made you think it was from her?"

"Because it said, 'Take me home.'" Bitty went on: "She can talk, but her voice is hard to hear 'cause she's so small. I think the rest of them talk too, 'cause someone must have taught her. I bet they're happy here, living with Grandma and Grandpa. That's probably why she wanted to come back."

Bitty smiled up at him. "You didn't believe me, did you, Troy? But now you know she's real."

"I don't know what to believe," Troy said. Yet there was something important in what Bitty had told him; he was sure of it. He reached over and put one hand on his little sister's head. "You're special, Bitty. Not many girls would make friends with a bug."

"Do you really think so?"

"Yes."

"I'm special," Bitty whispered. Her eyes sparkled.

"I think I need to go lie down," Troy said. His head was

pounding. He stretched out on the floor and pulled a blanket over himself.

He couldn't sleep. The clues came wafting in and out: the tiny handwriting, the letter from Friends of Pops and Earlene's, the R's on the envelopes that held the donations, the way the bug had appeared when he'd started playing, and the other one who'd pulled it back. *"I bet they're happy here . . ."* Bitty had said. What if the roaches had found out the club was in trouble? If it had been auctioned off, they might have had to move too. *Don't be ridiculous*, Troy told himself. And yet . . .

Troy had a sudden thought. He got up quietly. Bitty had fallen asleep across the bottom of the double bed. He found a scrap of paper and a pen on Grandma's bureau. Feeling foolish, he wrote in the smallest letters he could: For Shinola. Inside the paper he put a message with two questions:

Are you a roach? Did you and the others raise money for the club? Please check:

☐ *no*
☐ *yes*

Thanks, Troy
P.S. I can keep a secret.

He folded the paper into a tiny lump, went into the bathroom, and shoved it through the crack where the bug had disappeared.

༄༅

The Troy Wiggins Trio

TROY WAS ASLEEP WHEN the rest of the family came upstairs: first his mom and grandma, and later, around four in the morning, Charlie and Pops. Charlie had already driven to the twenty-four-hour teller and deposited more than thirty thousand dollars into the account the DJs had set up. He asked Pops about the money from the desk drawer in the office.

"I don't know who sent it. For a long time I didn't really think that it could be for me. Then yesterday I got a note from people who called themselves Friends of Pops and Earlene's. It said the money was mine to pay off the club's debts."

"You should have taken it to the bank!"

"It was already closed."

"What about the ATM?"

"I wasn't about to put all that in a machine."

"Well, you nearly lost it." Charlie described the robbery attempt. Pops was silent. The money was in the bank now, and this night he certainly wasn't about to contemplate the things that *almost* went wrong. He took off his shoes and lay back on the bed. Bitty was sleeping at his feet. Troy had curled up in a blanket on the carpet. Pops wondered what had happened to the trumpet.

To tell the truth, the flute suited Troy. Pops remembered how his grandson's music had streamed across the room downstairs, how it had felt alive in every nerve and joint and organ of his body. He remembered the day that he himself had tried to play for Louis Armstrong. He'd been too scared to get out a good note. Troy was scared too, but the music was stronger than his fear. Pops had known stars who said, "I wanted to quit playing so I could make a decent living, but the music wouldn't let me." When you felt it that way, you couldn't choose another life. Twenty years from now, he and Earlene would be gone, but Pops could imagine new names on the marquee under the pink saxophone outside: THE TROY WIGGINS TRIO. Maybe people from New York and Philadelphia would be lined up at the front door to pick up tickets. The neighbors' kids and grandkids would be there too, tapping their feet, listening to jazz.

"Good night, Dad." Charlie interrupted Pops's daydream. He put one hand on Pops's shoulder, and this time Pops put his own hand right on top of Charlie's.

"Good night, son. And thanks. Thanks for everything."

He watched Charlie go into the living room and lie in the recliner. Zeena was asleep on the couch. Pops didn't want to sleep. In fact, he wanted the day to last as long as it could. He lay on the bed, smiling. After a while Earlene stirred. She looked up and saw him there beside her.

"Herbert," she murmured.

"Did you like it?"

"I loved it. It was one of the best days of my life."

"We made a lot of money. I could take you on a little vacation, if the doctor says that it's okay. We could go to Florida or New York City."

She considered the idea.

"No, thanks."

"Why not?"

"I like it here."

"Did you ever wish I'd had a different job so we could have had more money? I could have been a mailman, or—"

"Of course not. We've had hard times, but look at us— we accomplished something. Think of all the people who loved our music."

Pops nodded. "I'm a lucky man," he said. Earlene didn't answer. She was drifting back to sleep.

Pops thought of the phone call offering the benefit, of the folks who'd schemed and planned to make the party what it was. He thought of his neighbors with their trays of food. He thought of the money from the R groups, the Friends of Pops and Earlene's. Why had they helped him? Would he ever find out who they were?

He sighed. From the side of his bed he could see

everyone he loved: Earlene, Charlie, Zeena, the grandkids. He remembered tonight's music. A wonderful peace settled over him. Thank you, Louis Armstrong, he thought. I wish you'd stayed alive to see how things turned out. He leaned over and switched off the light.

CHAPTER SIXTY-FOUR

Yes or No?

"IT'S ADDRESSED TO ME! I get to open it!" Shiny was beside herself. She'd never received a piece of mail before. Demo and Impy, standing behind the wall in the upstairs bathroom, looked at each other and shook their heads. What was Shiny getting herself into now?

But they were curious, too. They helped her unroll the scrap of paper and read the note.

Are you a roach? Did you and the others raise money for the club? Please check:

         ☐ *no*
         ☐ *yes*

Thanks, Troy
P.S. I can keep a secret.

Shiny wanted to answer Troy's questions that minute, but Impy said maybe they ought to stop and think about the consequences. After all, their trip up the drainpipe to the apartment the night before hadn't ended exactly the way they'd thought it would. Shiny hadn't apologized for the dancing escapade, or thanked Impy for pulling her back. While they were gone, Carlita had told the whole community the story of Demo and Do-zen, and how they'd saved Pops's money. The roaches had set a day of mourning and remembrance for Do-zen. When they'd started clapping for Demo, he'd felt so shy and overwhelmed that he hadn't been able to say a word.

Shiny kept gazing at the letter. "Shut up, Imp!" she said finally. "It's not addressed to you, so you can't tell me what to do."

"You're talking to an FB*R*I agent. And a hero! You should listen to what we think."

"How come? Checkmarks aren't a life-and-death decision."

"But if Troy knows that we helped Pops—"

"He can keep a secret."

"That's what he says now. What if he changes his mind?"

"Who's going to believe him?"

"Pops knows that something strange went on. He got all that money, and he still doesn't know who sent it."

"Who's going to believe *him* if he claims that roaches helped him? Everyone will say he's nuts."

"What do you think, Demo?"

"No check."

"That's it! I'll just check no and sign my name."

"But that's lying," Impy argued. "If you're going to check anything, it should be yes."

"Okay, I'll check yes." Shiny danced a little tango with her two hind legs. Then she showed Demo and Impy the green spot on her wing. She was sure that it was getting bigger.

Demo watched as she picked the note back up. "No check," he repeated.

"Shut up, Demo. You may be a hero, but I agree with Impy: it's wrong to lie. So I will tell the truth."

So she checked yes and signed the note *Love, Shinola Banan, "Miss Adventure."* She drew hearts and curlicues to dot her *i*'s. Then she folded the paper as small as she could and poked it back into the crack, so that just a tiny bit of it was

showing. Someone would have to look in that precise spot to notice it.

"When do you think Troy will be back?" she asked.

Nobody knew.

"I'm going to wait right here until he comes."

"I'm not. He might not come for several days. I'd get really hungry sitting here. Anyway, I told some of the Maddie nymphs I'd join their team for kick-the-crumb. They're practicing this afternoon."

"Kick-the-crumb." Demo nodded.

"If you both leave, I'll be here all alone."

"Then come with us."

"Shut up, Imp!"

The other two were starting down the drainpipe. Shiny watched their tails until they'd almost disappeared. Then she yelled, "Wait up!"

The tails slowed down. She jumped onto the pipe and hurried after them.